Daisy Morrow: Super-sleuth!

The First One:

The Root of All Evil

R T GREEN

Other books...

The Daisy Morrow Series:

The second one – The Strange Case of the Exploding Dolly-trolley
The third one – A Very Unexpected African Adventure
The fourth one - Pirates of Great Yarmouth: Curse of the Crimson Heart
The fifth One – The terrifying Tale of the Homesick Scarecrow
The sixth one – Call of Duty: The Wiltingham Enigma
The seventh one – Christmas in the Manor Born
The eighth one- The Shanghai Shadow
The ninth one – Some Like It Tepid
The Throwback Prequel: When Daisy Met Aidan
The Box Set – books 1-3
The Second Box Set – books 4-6 plus the Prequel

The Sandie Shaw series:

Book 1 – Murder at the Green Mill
Book 2 – Christmas in Chicago is Murder
Book 3 – An American in Windsor

The Starstruck Series -

Starstruck: Somewhere to call Home
Starstruck: The Prequel
(Time to say Goodbye)
Starstruck: The Disappearance of Becca
Starstruck: The Rock
Starstruck: Ghosts, Ghouls and Evil Spirits
Starstruck: The Combo – books 1-3

The Raven Series –

Raven: No Angel!
Raven: Unstoppable

3

Raven: Black Rose
Raven: The Combo – books 1-3

Somewhere Only She Knows
Timeless
Ballistic
Cry of an Angel
The Hand of Time
Wisp
The Standalones

As Richie Green –

Pale Moon: Season 1:

Episode 1: Rising
Episode 2: Falling
Episode 3: Broken
Episode 4: Phoenix
Episode 5: Jealousy
Episode 6: Homecoming
Episode 7: Fearless
Episode 8: Infinity

Season 2:

Episode 9: Phantom
Episode 10: Endgame
Episode 11: Desperation
Episode 12: Feral
Episode 13: Unbreakable
Episode 14: Phenomenal
Episode 15: Newborn
Episode 16: Evermore

TABLE OF CONTENTS

COME AND JOIN US

We'd love you to become a VIP Reader.

Our intro library is the most generous in publishing!
Join our mail list and grab it all for free.
We really do appreciate every single one of you,
so there's always a freebie or two coming along,
news and updates, advance reads of new releases...

Go here to get started...
rtgreen.net

Introduction

This is the first book in the Daisy Morrow series. Our R.E.D. heroine is nothing like you might expect; she's funny, feisty, and has a tendency to get herself in sticky situations. And she definitely has a wicked side!

Before she retired, Daisy had a job very few people ever have, and although in the last year she's done her best to leave her legacy behind, somehow it manages to keep lurking in the shadows... in more ways than one!

Those of you who know my work will be aware that with the RTG brand, the unexpected is always around the next corner. Daisy is no exception, and is very probably even more so.

I hope she will make you smile, and maybe even gasp in surprise and shake your head a little. If she does, it will make us happy!

Please let us know what you think, either by email, or ideally by writing a review. Every comment is gratefully received... and is listened to!

Enjoy,
Richard and the RTG crew

Daisy Morrow, Super-sleuth!

The Root of All Evil

Chapter 1

A quiet life in the country...

According to Daisy, nothing is ever quite what it seems.

Every time she comes out with that pearl of wisdom, Aidan shakes his head, shrugs his shoulders, and grins knowingly... if anything ever defied its appearance, it was surely her.

A smile creased her face as she drove slowly along the winding pedestrian path skirting the southern edge of the village duck-pond. A mid-morning August sun beat down out of a cloudless blue sky, and had already taken the temperature well into the twenties. The trip to the village shop had been made at just the right time; any later and it would have been seriously too hot.

She came to a stop, and watched the ducks for a few minutes as they swam lazily in the warm water. Calling it a duck-pond didn't really do it justice... it was more like a small lake, bordered on one side by trees and bushes, and the other flanked by the huge gently-sloping green, complemented by a couple of willow trees to enhance its tranquil beauty.

She moved to the village a year ago, after a very unfortunate incident in London made her decide country life might be the best option. Now she trundles around on a mobility scooter, even though she really doesn't need to.

That's not quite what it seems either... after three months of badgering Aidan because it 'didn't go fast enough', he finally succumbed to using his mechanical skills to make sure it did.

Adapting to rural Norfolk life went quite well, even though according to Daisy the village of Great Wiltingham is the "place people go to wilt".

That might be a little unkind. It's not entirely populated by retired folk... there are some families, and even a few young couples. But it has to be said the village has more elderly residents than anything else. It is a beautiful place to wilt after all, a second pond at the other end of the village, a lot of open green spaces, and the city of Kings Lynn just a few miles away.

The relentless sun reminded her it was time to find shade, so she screwed the throttle open and trundled to the pavement separating Walcotts Lane from the western edge of the pond. She'd left Aidan to unpack the new blender that arrived earlier, so there was no telling what that might lead to. The man was a genius when it came to engines and mobility scooters, but for some unfathomable reason his skills always seemed to desert him when faced with electric kitchen appliances.

The apprehension was justified. As she drove through the open five-barred gate and across the gravel towards the side door of the white-painted thatched cottage sitting on the opposite side of the road from the pond, through the wide-open kitchen window she heard the exclamation that usually meant something had gone drastically wrong.

14

'Bugger!'

She came to a stop next to the side door, the expletive from inside confirming there likely wasn't time to spend parking the dolly-trolley in its little open-fronted shack built as a lean-to next to the garage. Jesse's truck was in the drive, and as she grabbed her purchases from the basket fixed to the handlebars and headed quickly for the door, she nodded to his cheery wave.

'Good mornin' Mrs. M.,' he called out from the far side of the lawn. Jesse was the young village gardener, and given the advancing years of most of the population of Great Wiltingham, he never had to travel far to keep the work coming in.

'Good morning Jesse,' she answered politely, even though she was getting the feeling that at any moment it wasn't going to be a good morning.

As usual, she was right.

Aidan was just wiping the spots of strawberry-coloured goo from his face as she walked into the kitchen, and glanced around in dismay. His face wasn't the only thing covered in splatters of strawberry-coloured goo.

'Damn modern infernal kitchen appliances,' he growled.

'Blenders are hardly the stuff of ground-breaking technology, dear,' she grinned, despite the rather red appearance of the area in the kitchen where the infernal appliance was sitting. 'But I do believe you're supposed to put the lid on before you fire it up.'

'Oh is that what you do?' he glared at her, grabbing another wad of kitchen towel.

'No need for sarcasm, dearest,' she grinned back.

'I only switched it on for a moment, to make sure it worked.'

15

She ran some warm water over a cloth, and began to clean the spatters of strawberry and avocado from places they should never be. 'It's a super-duper turbo-boosted state-of-the-art mega-blender, dear. Might have been best to make sure it worked before you filled it to the brim?'

He finally smiled, as she wiped a tiny splatter from his nose. 'Well, at least I know it works now.'

Daisy shook her head, but still had to stifle a giggle for the sake of the slightly-disgruntled Aidan. She looked him and his once-white shirt over. Tall and slender, his short silver-grey hair had a tendency to flop a little over his forehead when he was flustered. Now seventy-six, his hair had migrated from absolute black quite a few years ago, but the occasional flop over the forehead had never changed, right from when she first met him almost forty years ago.

It was a silly insignificant thing that wasn't insignificant at all, because it was one of the little things that helped her fall in love with him. In truth, he had a lot of those little things, which carried on helping her stay in love with him to this day.

Including exasperating little matters like struggling with kitchen appliances.

She slapped him gently and lovingly on the shoulder. 'Quite like the tie-dyed red patches on the shirt, actually.'

'Very funny. But the splattered look is quite trendy right now, I hear.'

Daisy was about to retort something, but a strange, vaguely-tuneful noise coming from somewhere outside stopped the wit in its tracks. 'What on Earth is that? It sounds like a demented pigeon,' she said instead.

Together they walked towards the front window. And then they could both see the source of the strange noise.

'Oh dear,' said Aidan.

16

'I think it's me she wants,' said Daisy as she headed to the front door, lifting her eyes to the ceiling as she went.

The diminutive, slightly-portly woman was still cooing away at the gate as Daisy opened the front door. *'Cooeee... cooeee, Daisy?'* she called, waving an arm around to emphasise the shriek.

'Maisie... what the hell are you doing?'

She stopped cooing and waving. 'Well... I didn't want to disturb you...'

'So standing at the front gate cooing at the top of your voice and waving like a moron isn't disturbing me... and half the population of the immediate area?'

'Well, I... um...'

'Just come in Maisie, before the men in white coats arrive.'

'Oh... you don't really think...'

'No Maisie. Just winding you up. It is the easiest thing in the world, after all.'

The elderly woman trotted over to the door. 'There's no need to be so insulting...'

About to say the truth was never insulting, Daisy thought better of it, and instead just closed the door behind the woman in the nineties skirt and flower-patterned polyester blouse.

'I would offer you a strawberry and avocado smoothie, but you'd have to scrape it off the walls first.'

'I'm afraid I didn't understand any of that, Daisy.'

'Never mind. Tea?'

Aidan gave them a slightly-pained smile as they wandered into the kitchen. 'Ah, Maisie and Daisy, the terrible twosome of Wiltingham!'

17

Maisie didn't look too amused. 'Don't you start.'

'Just put the kettle on, dear,' said Daisy. 'And remember to close the lid first.'

He lifted a finger to waggle a visual retort to accompany words that never came, as he realised he was outnumbered, and that shutting up might be the better option. And he did close the kettle lid after he filled it.

Daisy and Maisie sank their butts onto their usual stools next to the island unit. 'So what can I do for you, Maisie?' said Daisy.

'Well dear... it's the strangest thing. Sometime in the night, my floribunda got uprooted.'

'Never heard it put quite that way before.'

Maisie lowered her head. 'It's not funny, Daisy. It's my pride and joy; I've lovingly cultivated it for years.'

Realising how upset she was, Daisy put an arm around her shoulders. 'I'm sorry, Maisie. My wicked sense of humour precedes my brain kicking in sometimes. But I don't see how I can help with a stolen rose bush?'

Maisie looked up, a gloss of tears in her eyes. 'Oh no dear, it hasn't been stolen. It's still there.'

Chapter 2

Daisy glanced curiously to Aidan as he placed two mugs on the island unit. He shook his head slightly, just as puzzled as she was.

'Maisie, you said it had been uprooted... but then someone *left it there*?'

She wrapped both her small hands around the mug, and took a sip like a little girl confessing something to the headmistress. 'Well, yes. It's... kind of still planted, but not like it was.'

'I think you'd better tell us the whole story, Maisie.'

'There's not much to tell. As I said, it's my special rose... each evening I water it, and wish it goodnight. Just like last night. Then this morning I noticed it was leaning a bit, and when I went and looked closer, I could see it had been dug up, and...'

'And?'

'Kind of... planted again, but not properly, like someone was in a hurry.'

'In a hurry... to replant a rose bush in the middle of the night, for no apparent reason?'

Maisie shook a rather sad head. 'I know it sounds crazy. I've done my best to replant it properly, but it's a bit delicate, you know. It won't be very happy.'

Daisy glanced up to Aidan, who was also shaking his head again, for an entirely different reason. 'Are you sure it wasn't some kind of weird dream, Maisie?' he said in a disbelieving kind of way.

She threw him an angry glance. 'I know half the village thinks I'm a dozy old biddie, but I'm not as crazy as I look. Then again, after this...'

Daisy pulled her into a hug. 'Take no notice of Aidan, he's just a man... I believe you Maisie, although it is a bit out of the box.'

'Thank you, Daisy. But... what do I do now? If it happens again, that'll be the end of my prize floribunda.'

Aidan turned away so Maisie wouldn't notice the grin on his face, but Daisy had a frown on hers. 'I'm not sure...' Then she had a sudden thought. 'Jesse... he's here right now. Maybe our village gardener could throw some light on it.' She slipped off the stool and headed to the side door, but then stopped in her tracks as the sound of his truck moving off filled her ears. She ran outside, just in time to see it turning out of the drive, and disappearing behind the trees.

She turned round to face Maisie and Aidan, who had followed her out. 'Oh well, next time I see him I'll pick his brains, ask if he's got any idea why someone would steal a rose bush but then not steal it. It isn't like him to go and leave the gate open though.'

Aidan nodded his agreement, and swung the big white gate shut. Maisie said she had to go give her prize floribunda some TLC, and disappeared through the little pedestrian gate next to the big one. Aidan threw Daisy his silly lopsided grin as he walked back over to her.

'You think the silly old biddie has finally lost it, dear?' he said.

'You can be so cruel sometimes, Aidan,' she replied.

'Oh, and you can't?'

'I'm quite capable of being far more wicked than you. But this time... well, this time I'm not so sure.'

He narrowed his eyes. 'So you're saying you think the village has a ghost gardener, who replants flowers in the middle of the night just to freak people out?'

20

'Maybe.'

'Oh come on, dear. I'm not Mulder, and you're sure as hell not Dana Scully!'

'Maybe we're not in an episode of the X-files here, but Maisie was well upset. And she knows her garden better than most. I think you should pop in and make sure she's ok first thing in the morning... and that the ghoulish gardener hasn't visited again, of course.'

He ambled back to the kitchen, shaking his head every step of the way. But Daisy knew he would do as she'd asked, because he was just that kind of guy. She followed a few steps behind, a slight frown on her brow.

Maisie was the nearest thing the village had to a crazie, but in reality she wasn't crazy at all. A little eccentric maybe, because she didn't do things quite the way everyone else did. Something Daisy could relate to, and definitely excuse.

Over the last few months they'd become friends, and once she'd forced her way through the eccentricities others saw as definitions of crazy, it was clear Maisie was just as sane as the rest of them.

Not that it said much for the rest of them.

But despite Aidan's initial head-shaking, she'd taken the time to understand her new friend. And one thing she'd discovered was that Maisie knew every inch of her garden. The floribunda in question was her pride and joy, but the same could be said about the whole of her garden.

If Maisie was convinced someone had been messing with her flora and fauna, then they probably had.

The *why* might be a little harder to work out though.

Chapter 3

Aidan turned up at ten the next morning. He spent the vast majority of his time at Daisy's, but he officially lived in a small bungalow just around the corner, in the leg of Walcotts Lane that branched off the part that skirted the pond. His street really should have been named something different... but it was rural Norfolk after all.

Despite the fact they'd been married for thirty-five years, Daisy and her husband owned separate properties.

The very unfortunate incident in London three years ago, and the day job Daisy had before she retired, both of which were very likely connected, had convinced them a new life and a modified identity was called for.

For two years after it happened they'd fought reluctantly with both the aftermath and the options, but eventually it was clear only one alternative stood a chance of working long term. So a year ago they'd moved together but separately to Great Wiltingham, purchasing two houses just a few hundred yards from each other, and putting their wedding rings into a velvet box that never left Daisy's bedside table drawer.

Daisy reverted to Morrow, her maiden name, and as far as anyone in Norfolk knew, she and Aidan were simply the best of friends.

He had initially protested that Daisy would spend most nights alone, wanting to be there to protect her if the worst happened. But as she pointed out, she was far more equipped to protect herself than he was. In the end he grudgingly accepted that, given the situation, she was probably right.

Aidan had spent his adult life working as an accountant.

Daisy hadn't.

'So any more ghost gardeners?'

He grinned as he walked through the kitchen door. 'Fortunately no, but I don't think Maisie got much sleep last night. I spotted a pair of binoculars amongst the ornaments on the window sill.'

'Poor thing.' She handed him a tall glass. 'Here, I made you a strawberry and avocado smoothie.'

'Now you're just proving a point.'

She grinned in the wickedest way possible. 'See it as you will, splatter-man.'

He took a sip. 'Calling me that, you've left me no option over which way to see it.'

'Maybe. But is it any good?'

'Delicious. And I can't see a single splatter on the tiles.'

She grinned at the sense of humour that was almost as wicked as hers. 'So how is the dear old biddie?'

'A little freaked out. She showed me the rose-in-question. It's in her front garden, which like most of the bungalows along there, is open to the road. Anyone walking past could have taken a fancy to it.'

She frowned at the hidden implication in his words. 'So you believe she hasn't gone completely crazy now?'

He managed to nod as he took another sip of the brew. 'I think I do, despite my reservations. If it had been just any old rose she hardly threw a second glance at for days at a time, I might have felt different, but...'

'One you kiss goodnight before you go to bed every night puts a different spin on it, yes?'

He laughed. 'To be fair, she only told us she *says* goodnight.'

'Never thought I'd see the day when you defended her.'

'Let's just say those who know every little quirk of the ones they love also know when something is different. Maisie loves her garden, and that rose in particular.'

'That was my thinking too. Could it have been a stray dog, or a fox?'

He kind of shook and nodded his head at the same time, making the lock of silver hair fall over his forehead. 'It's possible. But I can't see an animal uprooting a floribunda and then planting it again.'

'Hmm... nor me. But it still begs the question why.'

He raised a puzzled hand in the air. 'It's a brain-boggler for sure. Even if someone got disturbed when they were stealing it, they wouldn't have bothered replanting it again.'

Daisy filled the blender jug with warm water, and then let out a giggle. 'Are you listening to us? We're brainstorming the fact a rose bush didn't actually get stolen? Hell dear, we're turning into Norfolk country bumpkins for sure!'

He grinned. 'Maybe so... but I do like the Times crossword!'

'So you're saying this is something we have to spend hours doing, which has no actual benefit at all?'

He walked over to her, kissed her on the forehead. 'Not exactly. But you do have a point. Then again, aren't you curious to know the whys and wherefores of something that clearly happened, but has no obvious benefit to anyone?'

'Of course I am... but I'm not sure how to actually go about it.'

'I might have an idea.'

'Oh dear, dear. I know that look...'

For a moment he seemed reluctant to speak, but in that moment Daisy knew exactly why. 'I take it you brought the tech from London?'

He nodded. 'I was reluctant to raise the subject, but...'

Suddenly she was holding him tight, the gloss of tears in her eyes. 'It's ok, darling. It was three years ago, and it's starting to seem like it was in another life, even though it never will be. The night-vision camera never helped with Celia, but maybe it could assist us to solve a little puzzle now?'

He wiped away his own tear. 'Maybe,' he said quietly. 'From the bay window in my living room I can see right down the street. Maisie's place is only a few doors down, but on the off-chance whoever it was tries the same thing in another garden in that street, the camera will pick it up.'

'Back in London we rigged it to turn on a light to warn us if anyone came into range. Could we do something the same now?'

'Yes. I can rig it to switch on my bedside lamp. If I point the camera down the road and set it to run from midnight, I might at least get some sleep if Foxy doesn't go foraging too much.'

'It's a very slim chance it would happen again in the same street, but I can't believe you'd do this for Maisie.'

'You know me better than that, dear. But it's not just about Maisie. Between the pair of you, you've fired up my curiosity. It may be an insignificant little thing, but now it's puzzling the hell out of me!'

Chapter 4

Daisy didn't get a lot of sleep that night. Nothing was any different in the cottage... as always her phone was on the bedside table, and everything was as silent as it always was once the residents of the village went to bed.

The word sleepy definitely described Great Wiltingham. It was like the entire population hibernated after ten in the evening. On the occasional night she would hear a car drive past, but once midnight came not a sound broke the tranquillity.

Not from the human population anyway. Now and again the quack of a duck drifted through the open window, and even less occasionally when she couldn't sleep, a rustling in the bushes told her Foxy was on the prowl.

But that night, in the long periods punctuated by bursts of fitful sleep, not a single sound disturbed the peace. She'd told Aidan to ring her if anything happened, and somehow that knowledge was persuading her subconscious it was better not to sleep. The bad memories didn't help either. The man she loved had brought the surveillance tech with him, but not told her he had; the same tech they'd used back in London to try and shed light on the mystery that still didn't have closure.

Now he'd told her, and somehow that had made the events of three years ago seem like yesterday.

That hadn't exactly encouraged sleep either.

At three in the morning she ambled to the kitchen, made herself a cup of tea, and then padded into the garden. It was a hot summer night, almost stifling. A full moon cast its spotlight across the rear lawn, illuminating the trees and bushes in a ghostly and yet soothing light as she sat quietly at the table on the terrace, sipping her drink.

She allowed her thoughts free rein, even though some of them were hard to think. The hard ones came every day anyway, by choice. Without closure on what happened three years ago, most days she hit the PC in a so-far fruitless search for that closure.

She would never stop until she found it, one way or another.

Life in the village couldn't be more different to life in London. Yet even after she retired eleven years ago, her former employment didn't seem to want to let her be. She did make a few enemies after all. A while afterwards, the message seemed to get around that she'd left the life, and for a number of years her retirement fell into a relatively peaceful routine.

But then that peace came to an abrupt, and rather violent end. Daisy didn't suffer physical harm, that was never their intention. But the emotional harm for both her and Aidan was far worse, and a lot harder to repair.

Those responsible were eventually brought to justice. But Daisy was all too aware the people behind bars had plenty of loyal friends who weren't.

And because of the end result that was way too close to home, it was very likely there would never be an end at all.

Daisy forced her thoughts to the there-and-then. Aidan's good heart had overpowered his reservations, as she knew it would. And the desire that matched hers to solve puzzles was a pretty sure guarantee he would try all he could to discover why an innocuous rose bush was disturbed in the middle of the night, for no apparent reason.

She smiled to herself, picked up her phone from the wooden table, and headed back inside. She'd almost willed it to burst into life, with Aidan on the other end telling her the ghost gardener was working away further down the street.

But willing something didn't make it happen, as she knew all too well. In less than an hour the sky would lighten in the east, as a new day announced its imminent arrival.

If anything was going to happen, the chances were it wouldn't be that night.

She snuggled herself back into bed, and turned out the light. Maybe it would still be possible to get a couple of hours sleep before Aidan wandered round.

'No action then?'

'Not a sniff. Or a wisp maybe.'

Daisy smiled, gave him a kiss. 'You still think the village has a ghost then?'

He laughed. 'It's as good a theory as anything else right now. I even watched the tape back on times thirty-two. But we can't survey the whole village. Any of that smoothie left?

She lifted out a covered tumbler from the fridge, placed it on the worktop. 'Saved it just for you. On one condition...'

'You want breakfast?'

She nodded. 'Yes please. Being awake most of the night seems to have left me starving.'

'You didn't...'

'Just a little. Mostly my subconscious was waiting for you to ring.'

He pulled out the bread from its container. 'Must confess I spent some of the night watching out of my bay window, even though I knew the system would wake me if anything happened. It was like watching paint dry.'

'Never mind, dear. Maybe we should give it three or four nights, and then put it down to a one-off.'

He nodded as he grabbed a couple if items from the fridge. 'Maybe. Hellishly puzzling though.'

Daisy flicked the kettle, made them both a coffee, and then sat on her stool next to the island unit. A minute later a plate was plonked in front of her.

'Tuck in, darling. Welsh Rarebit, just as you like it, with pepperoni and jalapenos!'

She shook her head. 'Dearest, do stop calling it that... you sound like a wrinklie. Just say cheese on toast.'

'Well I would, except it's more like pizza.'

'Now you're splitting hairs.'

Chapter 5

They gave it three or four nights. It didn't make any difference. The ghost gardener refused to make an appearance. Aidan said he would leave the surveillance tech set up just in case, but he wasn't holding out much hope.

Daisy agreed, even though it was mystifying her just as much as it was Aidan. But then on the fourth morning something did happen, although it was nothing to do with night-time surveillance.

Daisy had driven to the local shop, as always on what Aidan affectionately called her dolly-trolley. As she walked through the door, someone was having a moan to the young woman behind the counter.

That in itself was hardly surprising, given who it was. Matilda was the village moaner, who seemed to be able to find a hundred things every day that didn't please her. A voracious member of the parish council, she was the self-styled high-standards warden of the village, making sure things that didn't need fixing got fixed anyway.

When Daisy first moved into her thatched cottage, Matilda was the one who insisted the trees which bordered the pedestrian pathway outside her house were cut back, so people walking past didn't get poked in the eye.

The only way anyone would get poked in the eye was if they were leaning through the trees to be nosy and see what was going on in the garden, but Daisy was a village newbie at the time, so meekly did as she was told.

These days she was quite prepared to tell Matilda where to go in no uncertain terms, but back then the last thing she wanted was to upset those who had been resident far longer than she had.

So when Matilda also told her she should keep her driveway gate closed at all times, she just smiled sweetly. She had no intention of leaving it open as an invitation to all and sundry.

Daisy often saw the village busybody in the store, sometimes buying a few bits, more often sticking some kind of notice on the board to tell people what they should and shouldn't do. It was one of life's unfortunate timings that Matilda and Daisy seemed to be out and about at the same time most mornings.

But this particular day, Matilda's wailing was more interesting than usual. Not the moan itself, more the person she was moaning about. Daisy tried to ignore the irritatingly loud voice, which managed to be both grating and squealy at the same time, and concentrated on the words instead.

'Well I don't know what to think, Sadie. I think he's just charging me for work that doesn't need doing. Since my husband died I don't have a lot of money, you know. And keeping an eye on the village takes all my time. He shouldn't take advantage of people like that.'

The young assistant smiled in a slightly-uninterested way. 'I've not heard anyone else complaining about Jesse's work, Matilda.'

'Well you know what British people are like, dear. We just don't complain enough.'

Daisy, keeping out of the way by idly examining the French sticks, found a rueful smile creeping over her face at Matilda's last statement. The same couldn't be said about everyone. But she hadn't finished ranting...

'Why, just this morning I looked out of my window and saw him replanting a rose bush in my front garden. I only asked him to do a bit of weeding. That rose was flourishing just as it was... he'll charge me for it, of course.'

'Maybe he felt it was necessary?'

'Absolutely not. People don't just replant roses for the sake of it. It's disgusting.'

'So did you say anything?'

'Of course I did. I went out and had a go at him. He tried to tell me it needed it. Load of nonsense, if you ask me.' She tucked her purchases into the capacious bag she was never seen without, and paid the assistant. 'He's gone to fleece someone else now, but when I get his bill I shall be deducting a sum for unnecessary work, mark my words. I'm now going.'

She flounced out of the shop, and didn't even pin something to the notice board.

Daisy noticed the assistant shake her head, and then their eyes met. 'Mornin' Daisy. How's you today?'

'Better than you, by the looks of it.'

'Oh, I get used to it from her. I just smile sweetly. Water off a duck's back, as they say around here.'

Daisy smiled at the very local inference of a well-known phrase. 'You think there's any truth to her moan?'

'Doubt it. Jesse's never upset anyone else... then again, he's only been here a couple of years. But if you're going to rile someone, it'll be Matilda.'

Daisy paid for the French stick, and a jar of locally-made jam. 'I've only been here a year, and I've already ruffled her feathers a few times.'

Sadie grinned. 'It's ok for you. I have to listen to every moan and groan, being here in the hub of the community, as it were.'

Daisy smiled back. 'Just remember what an invaluable service you provide for us old cronies, being a sounding board.'

'It's a dirty job, but someone's got to do it!'

32

Daisy trundled back towards home, but stopped again next to the pond. It was another beautiful day, and it looked like a couple of hundred ducks knew it too, dabbling away in the water in a lazy, unhurried kind of way.

But she wasn't really seeing them. Village busybody or not, Matilda's moaning was bouncing around her head like a rubber ball on steroids. Maisie's little incident was still taking up a big swathe of brain-power, and rose bushes featured strongly in that. Now it appeared Jesse the gardener was unnecessarily replanting another rose bush, a seemingly-unconnected fact of life that in Daisy's mind felt like it was somehow connected.

And the fact he was supposed to do some gardening for her yesterday but hadn't turned up, seemed to be yet another issue that was, or wasn't, connected.

But there was one question neither she nor Aidan had asked Maisie four days ago, because four days ago it hadn't even occurred to them. But suddenly it had become relevant, and Daisy being Daisy, it had to be asked right away.

She narrowed her eyes, and screwed open the throttle. Before she went home, there was a visit that must be made.

Chapter 6

Daisy placed the rose-patterned bone china cup back on its saucer, and decided it was time to ask Maisie the burning question.

Her prize floribunda didn't seem to have suffered from its altercation with the ghost gardener, but no one seemed any the wiser as to why it had been disturbed.

The binoculars were still on the window cill.

'Maisie, this might seem a random question, but was Jesse working here the day of the incident in the night?'

She thought for a moment. 'Why yes, he was. But I really don't think he would come back after dark and mess with my rose... at least not in the crude way it was.'

Daisy couldn't stop a slight giggle, which made Maisie frown. She waved an apologetic hand. 'Sorry dear, neither do I. Just a silly thing I heard in the village shop half an hour ago.'

'So are you going to tell me, or keep me in suspenders?'

'It's just that Matilda was in there...'

'That bossy cow?'

'Um... yes. Something she said, about Jesse working there this morning and replanting a rose, which in her opinion didn't need it.'

'She's far too opinionated if you ask me. She thinks I should move away, reckons I bring down the area.'

'Seriously? She told you that?'

'Well, not in so many words. But I'm not as crazy as I look. I know exactly what she's thinking.'

Daisy frowned. The daft part of her brain was just envisioning the perceived village crazie in the new light of the village telepath. She shook away the thought, before it

festered. 'Don't listen to her. And don't think things...
promise me?'

'I have to think some things, dear.'

'I meant... oh never mind. What was Jesse doing on your
garden?'

'Just a little weeding. My poor old back, you know.
Getting down and dirty is difficult. And he's young and quite
fit, after all.'

'Maisie?'

'Dear, my back might be past it but my thoughts aren't...
oh sorry, I'm not supposed to think, am I?'

'I didn't mean... oh, never mind. Did you watch him the
whole time?'

'That's a personal question, isn't it?'

'I meant... maybe I'm not making myself clear, Maisie.
But did you?'

'I watched him some of the time... he wears quite short
shorts, you know.'

'Maisie...'

'But no, not all the time. I was on the phone to my
sister... and then I made him a cup of tea.'

Daisy narrowed her eyes. 'I see.'

'Well I don't. Are you going to let me in on the secret?'

'No. Not yet. There isn't actually a secret right now. Just
a slightly-troubling thought...'

'You've been gone a while.'

Daisy found Aidan sitting on the terrace, reading a book
under the shade of the big green parasol. She sat down on
the chair next to him. 'I was eavesdropping on a
conversation in the village store... well, a rant really.
Matilda was bending Sadie's ear.'

'Ah, the resident village dragon breathing fire again.'

35

'Indeed. But it was the what she was saying that set me thinking. So then I went to see Maisie.'

He looked a little puzzled by her words, so Daisy told him all about the fire-breathing dragon's rantings. Then he looked puzzled for an entirely different reason.

'You think our gardener has something to do with this?'

'Don't you?'

'It seems more likely than not. He must have seen Maisie arrive here the other day, and known why she'd come. He did leave in rather a hurry, and then didn't turn up at all yesterday. That's suspicious if you look at it in a different light, but it still doesn't explain why he's replanting floribundas that don't need it.'

'No, it doesn't. But there has to be a reason.'

'I'll make us some lemonade.'

He headed back to the kitchen. Left alone with her thoughts, Daisy found them running rampant. And the location of the incidences was the first piece of the puzzle that seemed to fit.

Walcotts Lane was in three sections. The part of the road she lived on ran for half a mile or so, and then meandered off into the countryside. Fifty yards after her cottage, a road branched off at right angles. It looked like a separate road, but for some odd reason was still called Walcotts Lane. A hundred yards further on, just before the bungalow where Aidan lived, the road split again, into two parallel streets that from the air looked like the prongs of a tuning fork.

Both of these prongs, each called Walcotts Lane, ended in dead ends. And pretty much all the bungalows on both prongs had front gardens open to the road. Maisie lived a few doors further along from Aidan, on the right prong. Matilda lived halfway along the left prong.

36

If there was something suspect going on someone didn't want people to know about, that part of Walcotts Lane was surely the place to do it. No through traffic, and the majority of the residents getting on in years, and extremely unwilling to go out after dark.

But what was the suspect thing... and what had rose bushes got to do with it?

She voiced her thoughts to Aidan as he set down a tall glass of iced lemonade on the table in front of her. He didn't seem too surprised. 'The same thing occurred to me. But I'm still devilishly puzzled as to the what, and why.'

'Talking of devils, that's where the detail is.'

'I hope you're not saying what I think you're saying?' He looked into her eyes, and shook his head. 'You are.'

'Don't you think digging up Matilda's rose might give us answers? Jesse only replanted it a few hours ago, so if he left any clues they'll be fresh.'

'Can I finish my lemonade first?'

'Oh, you've got plenty of time, dear. If we're going to mess with the dragon's den, I'm not prepared to incur her fiery wrath over a hunch that might prove to be nothing. Would you fancy explaining to her why we're gate-crash gardening in someone else's garden? I don't want dear Matilda, or anyone else for that matter, to know what we're doing. Until we're sure there's a sound reason why we're doing it, anyway.'

'You mean...'

'After everyone's asleep, we'll raid the grounds. You ever done any midnight gardening, dear?'

Chapter 7

'You hiding a box of Milk Tray behind your back?'

'Well I was going to wear my orange visi-vest, but it was in the wash.'

'Very funny. But you do look like the Milk Tray man... apart from the silver hair.'

'And you look like... well, like you used to.'

'Don't remind me. I thought it appropriate wear for a commando raid on a rose bush.'

'It's all quite exciting, dear.'

Daisy shook her head, but didn't reply. Two minutes ago Aidan had opened the front door to let her into the bungalow, and as he'd looked her up and down, grinned at her attire. Likely because it was virtually identical to his. A black jumper and jeans, the only difference was the headgear... his a black baseball cap, hers a dark grey woolly bobble-hat.

She'd made the two-minute trek to his as the time clicked to nine in the evening. The sky to the west was still dark blue, the last diffused rays of the sun clinging onto the remains of the day. It was virtually dark, but not quite.

She was wary of making the trip along the secluded narrow alleyway when it was pitch black. Rural Norfolk was hardly London, but old habits die hard.

The alleyway didn't really shave much distance off the journey, but it was extremely useful when you didn't want all and sundry and Matilda to know just how much time you spent with someone. Just a few yards from Daisy's cottage at one end, it opened out at the other end in Walcotts Lane, right next to Aidan's bungalow.

It was one of the things that had sold him the property... the short, narrow, virtually-hidden pathway could have been made especially for their situation.

That particular evening it served another useful purpose. Dressed like cat woman in a bobble-hat, Daisy really didn't want to use the main walkway and risk running into someone who might have asked awkward questions. So she'd slunk along the pathway like a feral feline, slipped through Aidan's side gate which opened directly onto the pathway, and smiled a slightly-relieved smile when she saw him dressed in similar fashion.

'I suggest we don't make a move until midnight,' he said as he flicked on the kettle. 'I doubt there'll be anyone awake then, and no insomniac dog-walkers either, hopefully.'

'We are taking a bit of a risk though.'

'But it is Matilda we're talking about. As long as she doesn't discover us, I doubt anyone else who might spot us would incur her fire-breathing wrath by telling her.'

'If she sees us, she'll make sure no one in the village will ever forget who midnight-raided her floribunda.'

'Now I'm getting an image I don't want.'

'Be afraid. Be very afraid...'

'Just... just be quiet, dear, and drink your tea.'

'I brought my torch.'

Aidan glanced at the big silver cylinder in Daisy's hand as he closed the side door behind them. 'Just point it at the ground... if you wave that thing in the air it'll seem like the blitz again.'

'How would you know? You were just a glint in your daddy's eye then.'

'I've seen pictures.'

'Of torches?'

He shook his head, but seemed to be grinning. 'Of wartime searchlights... and if you point that thing upwards, that'll look just like one. I can imagine the rumours spreading through the village like wildfire... strange lights in the sky, aliens landing in Great Wiltingham...'

'You're such a dipstick, Aidan Henderson. But you do make me laugh when I need it.'

'Only when you need it?' he retorted as they reached the walkway and hurried across the road, turned left and then almost immediately met the sharp junction in the road that was the start of the left prong.

Not a light shone from a window. There was very little light from anywhere. Although one or two people had rigged up their own, streetlamps didn't exist in that part of the village. And a hazy cloud had drifted across the sky a few hours ago. They could just about see the moon, but it was a pale, diffused effigy of the bright spotlight it seemed to have been for the last four weeks.

It was like Mother Nature knew it wasn't really wanted that night.

The cloud cover had brought with it a faint, cool breeze. It felt like the long dry spell was coming to an end, and as they walked quickly towards their target, the dark, faintly-spooky hulks of the bungalows either side of them weren't helping the atmosphere.

'I've got goose bumps,' Daisy whispered.

'You?' Aidan whispered back. 'I thought this would be a walk in the park for you.'

'Plonker. I've never been on a midnight raid to dig up a rose bush belonging to a fire-breathing dragon before. Anyway, it's not the mission... it's just the chill in the air.'

'Sure it is. And please stop stage-whispering. Someone might hear.'

'You're stage-whispering too, Dipsy.'

'Only to answer you, Laa-Laa.'

'Shall I switch the searchlight on now? I think I can hear enemy bombers in the distance.'

'Daisy dear...' His words faded away as he realised they were right outside the fire-breathing dragon's lair. He glanced around furtively. It seemed they were the only two people in Norfolk right then. And the dragon's windows were shut, another slight bonus of the chilly night. 'Ok, but point it down to the soil.'

'Did you bring the trowel?'

'Damn, I knew I'd forgotten something.'

He shook his head as he pulled it out of the capacious inside pocket of his parka. Daisy panned the torch around the front garden. It was mostly bushes, but right in the centre was a patch of gravel, with a flower bed in the middle of that. It was almost covered by a mass of bright orange marigolds, except for the centre. That was dominated by the floribunda.

'That's got to be it,' whispered Aidan.

'You don't say.'

He ignored her grin, started to make his way through the bushes to reach the rose. Until he felt a restraining hand on his arm, and glanced up to see Daisy's grinning face. 'Be careful, dear. Knowing whose lair this is, those bushes might rear up and eat you.'

'Will you please be quiet?'

'Just saying...'

Together they made their way gingerly through the bushes. And Daisy did keep the torch on the ground. As they

41

knelt next to the rose, they could see straightaway it had been messed with. The beam threw a bright spotlight on the soil surrounding it. It looked like it hadn't been firmed properly, not the work of a professional gardener.

While Daisy ferreted around for any clues that might have been left, Aidan sunk the trowel into the ground next to the rose. He glanced up to her. It had slipped in far too easily. And the soil was bone dry.

Anyone replanting a shrub would have known the fact that, more than ever given the long dry spell, the first essential would have been to water it.

Especially the village gardener.

'Try lifting it up and back a little, dear. I'll get my hands underneath the roots,' Aidan whispered.

Daisy's leather-gloved hands grasped the stem, and she did as he asked. She didn't need to exert much effort, the rose moved easily. His hands disappeared into the cavity in the loose soil, and two seconds later he let out a whispered gasp.

'There's something here.'

Daisy couldn't see properly, the blooms and leaves in the way. But her heart began to pound. Aidan tended to say 'bugger' a lot, but he rarely gasped. A gasp meant something completely different. Something exceedingly spectacular.

As he lifted the package away from the roots, Daisy gasped too. It was wrapped in thick clear plastic to protect it, but it instantly switched her heart to overdrive. Not just because she already knew what it was, but because of the sheer size of it.

Aidan whispered the words, in a shocked, faltering kind of way. 'Now why would anyone bury a bag of flour underneath a rose bush?'

42

'I don't think it's flour, dear.'
'You don't say.'

Chapter 8

'I didn't quite expect that.'

Daisy took a large swig of the brandy Aidan had poured for her. She didn't look so good. Sitting opposite her at the small table in his kitchen, he too looked like he was still struggling to come to terms with what they'd found.

Not that Daisy was exactly looking at him too closely. Ever since they'd slumped down onto the pine dining chairs, she seemed unable to wrench her gaze away from the package that sat on the table between them, like it was the centre of the universe.

'Are you ok, darling?'

His words seemed to pierce the glass bubble which only contained her and the package. She finally glanced up, and forced a weak but unconvincing smile. 'I'll survive. It's just a bit... a bit of a shock, you know.'

'I did think we'd left all that behind,' he said quietly, and a little ruefully, reaching out a hand and wrapping it around hers.

She shook her head slowly, and called him by the affectionate nickname she sometimes used, which started so long ago neither of them could remember how it came about. 'We can never leave it behind, Dip. It's everywhere these days. But Great Wiltingham...'

'And such a massive quantity.'

'I've never seen so much in one package. Even when Celia...'

'Hey, don't even go there, ok? This is something else entirely.'

'Is it? We got the bad guys eventually, but not Mister Big. He's still out there somewhere.'

'Darling, there's a lot of Mister Bigs around. I doubt it's the same one.'

She swigged the last of the brandy. 'You filling that up again?' She lifted her head to the ceiling as she handed him the empty glass, trying to find some logical, or maybe divine thinking. 'You're right, dear. It's a remote possibility it's the same Mister Big... but Jesse?'

He grabbed the brandy bottle from the kitchen worktop, sat back down and refilled her glass. 'Sip it, dear,' he smiled. 'Getting pissed right now isn't going to help.'

She lowered her head. 'I know. Just bad memories, firecracking their way into my heart. And here, in the village?'

He nodded. 'A double whammy for sure. And Jesse has a lot to answer for. Clearly what he's doing is way beyond personal use, so he's without doubt a wholesale supplier in whatever county line he's mixed up in.'

Daisy's eyes fell back to the package. 'The root of all evil,' she said quietly. 'That's a fortune sitting there staring at us.'

Aidan found a laugh. 'It's actually us staring at it, if the truth be told. But staring isn't getting us anywhere. We should call the police.'

'Dear, it's two in the morning.'

'So?'

'So, we'll get a squad car popping round in a couple of hours, and two bored-out-of-their-skull officers asking difficult-to-explain questions, and then taking the package away and saying "someone will contact you later on".'

He shook his head, knowing exactly what was coming. 'I guess you're now going to tell me you've got a different strategy in mind?'

'Jesse lives on that small mobile home park at the other end of the village.'

'What, that ants' nest of seething humanity?'

'Don't be unkind, dear. There's a lot of struggling, out-of-work people around these days, with not much to do other than take an interest in what goes on around them.'

'I'm sorry. It's another world we're no longer part of. But that trailer park is still an ants' nest.'

'Yes dear. Exactly.'

He looked up, his eyes suddenly wide. 'Daisy... no...'

'It seems to me if Jesse is some kind of wholesale distributer, it's not the best idea to do it from where he lives, being spotted with a host of unsavoury characters who pop in regularly. Neighbours always seem to know what's going on. If, God forbid, I was doing what he was, I'd make sure my transactions were made well away from my home. And what better way to do it if you're the village gardener than to use your day job to make deliveries in secret?'

He nodded. 'I can understand that... but please don't say what I have a horrible feeling you're going to...'

'Tomorrow... sorry, today, is Sunday. I doubt he'll be working, especially given his night time job. I think we should pay him a visit, use that... very valuable package there as a bargaining chip to get him to talk, and maybe give up his bosses. Then we can involve the police.'

He narrowed his eyes, and gave her the knowing stare through his brows. 'Daisy... you do mean just... talk?'

'Don't worry, dear. Much as I'd like to, I won't take... anything with me. We'll just talk.'

'I don't like it. It's a dangerous world we're getting drawn into.'

46

Daisy smiled, not as convincingly as she could have. 'Oh come, dear... it's Jesse the village gardener we're talking about here. He's clearly got wrapped up in something way outside his comfort zone. We can use that to get him to spill.'

'I still don't like it. But I'm old enough and wise enough to know when you get that glint in your eye, not even I can stop you.'

'I suppose old habits die hard.'

He shook his head. 'Oh dear. Just promise me not all of them die hard, please?'

'Of course, dear.'

'Hmm... if we're going to tackle the bad guys later on, we should grab some sleep. I'll walk you back to the cottage, Daisy.'

She looked up to him, and he saw the gloss of tears in her eyes. 'Dear, please can I stay here? I... I don't fancy sleeping on my own tonight.'

He smiled, stood and took her hand. 'Of course. Let's go shuggle up.'

An hour earlier, Daisy and Aidan had hastily replanted the offending rose, and made sure there was no indication it had been uprooted yet again. Together they'd made their silent way back to the bungalow, both of them too shell-shocked for conversation, and too numb to notice something they maybe should have noticed.

But then again, a strange car parked a hundred yards from their route, right next to the entrance to the tuning-fork of Walcotts Lane, wasn't really that unusual.

But the dark SUV, and the man dressed in black sitting silently inside it, was very much a part of the dangerous world they were about to walk right into.

Chapter 9

The morning light filtered through a grey, overcast sky. It did nothing for the mood in Aidan's bungalow. It seemed to Daisy like the weather had latched onto her mood, and was matching it every step of the way.

Aidan threw her a concerned glance as they climbed into his BMW. He knew all too well the unexpected discovery of a few hours earlier had ripped a lightning bolt of memory through her heart.

He'd always been a laidback kind of guy, something that had helped him weather the storm of heartbreak back in London.

Daisy wasn't laidback.

'We just give him the bare facts of life, let them persuade him to tell us what we need to know, ok?' he said as he started the engine.

She threw him back a half-angry glare. 'Am I carrying any instruments of torture, Aidan?'

He couldn't see any, but he decided to shut up anyway. Daisy was strong-willed, and in the past had never shied away from using whatever means was necessary to achieve her objective... but at least this time he was there to intervene if things got out of hand.

To protect her from others... and from herself.

The trailer park was only a two-minute drive, tucked away behind a screen of trees and tall bushes about half a mile beyond the second village pond. Aidan thought to himself Matilda must have got her way when it was built four years ago. Right on the edge of the village, you couldn't even see the small park until you were right next to it.

He drove between the low walls of the open entranceway, and glanced again to Daisy. Her eyes were scanning the mixture of permanent and mobile homes there, her lips clamped together into a tight, determined pout. Other than the pout, she wasn't giving away what she was thinking.

It wasn't difficult to work it out though, when he knew her as well as he did.

There seemed to be people of all ages everywhere. It was ten on a Sunday morning after all, but in truth many of the residents there didn't have jobs to go to. A few people cast curious glances at the smart car driving slowly along the narrow access roads, and some kids playing together stopped what they were doing to try and see where it was heading.

'I told you it was an ants' nest,' said Aidan as he brought the car to a stop, and dropped the driver's window. 'Hey kids... we're looking for Jesse's caravan.'

A boy with a football in his arms, and a girl who looked like his sister, wandered over. 'What do you want Jesse for?' the girl asked, her eyes narrowed suspiciously.

'Um... we're friends of his. He does our garden.'

Daisy leant over. 'We've got something for him,' she smiled sweetly.

Aidan threw her a button it glance, but the young girl wasn't for budging. 'I don't think we should tell you.'

'Well, we could just drive around until we spot his truck.'

The girl glanced to her brother, who shrugged his shoulders. Then she lifted an arm, and pointed a finger. 'Go round there, just keep going. His van's right on the edge of the park.'

49

'Thank you!' Aidan gave them a cheery wave he certainly wasn't feeling, and drove away in the direction of the pointing finger.

They spotted the truck before they spotted the caravan. It was parked up against the perimeter bushes, with Jesse's slightly scruffy caravan between it and another wheeled caravan sitting next door.

'Well, he's here,' said Daisy matter-of-factly.

'Just remember what we said,' Aidan reminded her.

She threw him a smile without a trace of humour in it, grabbed her bag from the back seat, and opened the passenger door.

'If he's wholesaling drugs, why is he living like this?' asked Aidan as he climbed out to join her in the chilly morning air.

'Likely by choice. I very much doubt he actually has to, so he's putting up while he amasses the fortune to start a new life somewhere else.'

'All the more reason to stop him in his tracks while we still can, I guess.'

'You're not wrong, Dip.'

There didn't seem to be any signs of life as they walked over to the van, but then the door in the next caravan opened, and a woman stepped out with a basket of wet clothes. She headed for a short washing line draped between a thin metal pole and a hook fastened to the side of her caravan.

She dropped the basket on the ground and lit up a cigarette, glanced over. 'You lookin' for Jesse?'

'Yeah. He still asleep, given it's Sunday?'

50

'Not seen or heard a peep from him. Unusual though, he's normally up and playin' that rap music by now. He don't sleep late like some other folk.'

The last three words were screeched out, and aimed at someone who was clearly lazing his Sunday away inside her caravan. Daisy forced a grin. 'Men, huh?'

'Tell me about it.'

'Excuse me...' spluttered Aidan.

'Thanks anyway,' said Daisy to the woman. 'Guess I'd better wake him up.'

She balled her fist and thumped hard on the door. The thunderous noise didn't seem to have any effect, so she hammered again. 'Jesse... I know you're in there.'

Still nothing. Daisy turned to Aidan. 'The little toe-rag is panicking now, quaking in his boots. Break the door down, Aidan.'

'Excuse me? He might have just gone for a walk.'

'Nah. He's in there. You doing the necessary, or do I have to find a heavy log?'

'I don't know about this, Daisy...'

'Stop being such a wuss. He can afford to pay for the damage.' As she spoke, she idly wrapped her fingers around the door handle. It moved down, and the door swung open. 'Oh.'

'It's unlocked,' said Aidan unnecessarily.

'So it is.'

'Daisy, be careful... it might be a trap.'

Daisy had no intention of being careful. She thundered up the steps, and strode into the darkness of the caravan. Aidan hurried after her.

At one end of the van, a three-sided sofa wrapped around the walls. And sprawled out on one side, his feet on

51

the floor, Jesse was fast asleep. Daisy stomped up to him, kicked a leg.

'Hey you... wake up, I'm about to call the police.'

He didn't move. But as Aidan drew back a couple of the curtains and a grey light flooded in, they knew why. As Daisy turned away and put desolate hands to her face, he knelt down next to Jesse, and pulled back the lapel of his jacket.

'I think we really should call the police. He's been stabbed, dear.'

He stood back up, just as Daisy fell into his arms, and sobbed wretchedly into his shoulder. For a moment he held her tight and let her cry it out, and then, a little puzzled, he eased her back.

'Dear, what's wrong? It's not like you've never seen death before. I don't understand why you're so upset?'

She turned away, shook her head, and rubbed the tears from her eyes. 'Don't you see?' she said shakily.

'I see a dead man, who was doing very bad things.'

'Yes... and we're the ones responsible for getting him killed!'

Chapter 10

Aidan pulled the phone from his pocket, dialled 999. 'Do you think..?' He glanced to Daisy, and then answered the operator's words. 'Police, please. I'd like to report a murder.'

Whilst he gave her the details, Daisy pulled herself together, and examined the room. Then Aidan killed the call, and turned to her. 'Daisy?'

She shook her head. 'By the looks of it he's been dead several hours. Which only serves to confirm the fact we're responsible for him not living.'

'Are you saying..?'

She knelt down next to the corpse, and picked up some oblong slivers of notepaper, which looked like they'd been torn up and thrown at the body. 'Now we know what we do, it's not difficult to work out what went down here, is it Aidan?'

He lifted his hands from his sides, a sign that told her it really wasn't difficult. 'I guess we found the package before the person who was supposed to, which didn't make him very happy when he discovered nothing under the rose bush.'

Daisy tried to piece together the eight scraps of torn paper. 'For sure. So then he rushed here and confronted Jesse, thinking he was being double-crossed. Poor Jesse had no way to convince him otherwise, things got out of hand, and he ended up dead. We're talking about a huge amount of money here, after all.'

'Poor Jesse? He was the one helping to make it possible for god knows how many kids to ruin their lives.'

53

'I know, dear. But he didn't deserve to die because of us.'

He knelt down beside her, took her slightly-trembling hand. 'Maybe not. But we can't blame you and me, Daisy. He was the one dealing with evil, dangerous people. He must have known the risks. All we did was discover the package, and take it with us.'

'Maybe we should have left it where it was, watched to see who came for it.'

'And what then? Carry out a citizen's arrest on someone armed and willing to use a knife?'

Daisy shook her head. 'I don't know, dear. As soon as I saw what it was, I just needed it and us to get home. I wasn't thinking straight... and judging by your face, neither were you.'

He nodded his agreement. 'I will admit it shook me to the core. But thinking about it, if Jesse was arranging secret drops, he wouldn't want very valuable merchandise sitting in the ground too long. He'd stash it in someone's garden while he was working there in the day, for whoever it was to collect the same night.'

Daisy looked at him with wide eyes. 'Oh hell. Do you think whoever it was actually saw us?'

He lowered his head. 'Maybe. We didn't notice anyone, but we were a bit shell-shocked at the time.'

'Hmm... I think I'm more than a little rusty. My bad.'

'What's that you've got there?'

She gave up trying to piece the slivers together. 'They were scattered around the body. There's something written on them, but we'll have to take them home to see what it is. They're well ripped up.'

'Do you think the killer tore it up?'

'That's my thinking. In anger, and then threw the pieces at Jesse. So it must mean something.'

'We should really give them to the police.'

'Dear, we're going to hand them a large consignment of evil. We've got to keep something for ourselves.' She slipped the little pieces into the pocket of her coat, and then lifted her head and listened. 'Talking of police...'

The scream of a wailing siren in the distance grew louder as they listened. In less than a minute, they would be far from alone.

The pretty young constable sat down at the small built-in dining table opposite Daisy. A few minutes ago, Aidan had shifted the remains of the Papa John's pizza to clear the top so they could use it. The girl in the pristine black uniform put her notebook and pen onto it, and tried to smile a reassuring smile to the silver-haired lady who looked totally bemused by the whole situation.

'This must be very upsetting for you, Mrs. Morrow.'

'It's Daisy, dear,' said Daisy, wiping away a tear that she'd made herself shed. It hadn't been that hard to find one.

'My name is Constable Sarah Lowry. Is it okay to ask you a few questions?'

'That's a very unusual first name, dear.'

'I'm sorry?'

'Constable... there's not many girls with that name.'

'Oh... no, you don't understand, Mrs... Daisy. My first name is Sarah, my designation is constable.'

'Oh, now I see. So why didn't you just say that?'

'Um... I don't deal with many... um...'

'Old people, dear?'

'Senior citizens, I prefer to call them... you.'

55

'How old are you, Constable Sarah?'

The clearly-inexperienced woman with the natural blonde hair tied up into a bun just about as tight as it would go, looked down to the pen in her slender hands. I... um... I'm twenty-three.'

Daisy sighed deliberately. 'So young to be dealing with dead bodies.'

She noticed Aidan in the background, shaking his head in a slightly-amused way. The young woman who reminded Daisy of someone, didn't look as amused. 'If you must know, it's my first murder case.'

'Oh my dear, I'm so sorry. But I guess it had to happen sooner or later. How long since you've been out of the academy?'

'Um... six months.'

'Six months...' Daisy lifted her eyes to the slightly-dingy roof of the caravan. Not for the reason the young officer thought... more about the fact that if she'd been in London her first murder case would have been six hours after graduation, not six months. 'So you're still wet behind the ears then.'

'I'm sorry?'

'It doesn't matter. So what made you choose a career in the police, dear?'

'I... Daisy, it's supposed to be me asking the questions.'

Daisy put a finger to her head, just like Columbo when the penny dropped. 'Oh... I am so sorry, dear. You know what us wrinklies are like...'

A slight smile curled the woman's full lips upwards. 'It's ok. But I'm a bit puzzled. How come you were here in the first place, and discovered the body?'

'Ah well, you see, it's like this. Jesse does my garden for me, and my friend Aidan's too...' She waived a slightly-shaky hand in his direction. 'And he also does my friend Matilda's. She was moaning something about him replanting one of her roses when it didn't need it, and so we went to see what all the fuss was about, and then we saw he hadn't done it properly, so we lifted it out to replant it, and found something he must have forgotten in the soil underneath it, so then we decided to bring it back to him, and...'

'Daisy... slower, please.' Sarah was scribbling furiously on the notepad, desperately trying to keep up with the barrage of words.

'Sorry, dear. It's all so upsetting, you know. And puzzling too. Perhaps I should just give you what we brought Jesse back, so you can see what you make of it.'

Daisy rummaged around in her bag for a few moments longer than really necessary, and then slapped the package onto the table.

'Why anyone would want to bury a bag of flour underneath a rose bush is beyond me!'

Chapter 11

The young constable's flawless blue eyes opened wide. Hesitantly she picked up the package, and turned it around in her hands like she couldn't quite believe what had been slapped on the table.

'Is it some kind of flour, dear?'

'Um... we'll have to get it to the lab, run a few tests, Daisy.'

'Might be best not to hang around doing that, dear.'

Her big eyes flicked back to the senior citizen sitting opposite her, and narrowed into a questioning frown. But then someone walked up to them. 'Lowry, we need to get these people out. Forensics are here, and this is a major crime scene now.'

'Yes, sir.' She stood up, and straightened the pristine uniform. 'Would you like a hand, Daisy?'

Daisy struggled to her senior citizen's feet, and gasped out the words. 'I think I can manage, thanks dear.' She cast her eyes over the burly man who had barked out his instructions. He was clearly much more experienced than his rookie partner, judging by the emotionless eyes sunk into his fifty-something face, and the nicotine stains on the fingers of both hands. 'Who are you, anyway?' she asked in a faltering voice.

He grunted out the words. 'DCI Burrows, Mrs. Morrow. I'm in charge of this investigation.' His hollow eyes fell onto the package on the table. 'For the time being, anyway.'

Daisy made her slow, painful way out of the caravan. People in white coveralls were already assembling a blue canvas tent ready to sit up against the door, and as she made it down the steps and looked slowly around, a large crowd of curious park residents had already assembled on the far side of the narrow road.

She smiled to the humourless DCI. 'So can we go now, Detective Chief Inspector?'

He lifted his hands from his sides. 'I suppose so. But we'll need to talk further in the near future. Just don't leave town.'

'Which town, Inspector?'

He glared at her. 'Ok... don't leave the village.'

'Can I still go to the shop on my mobility scooter?'

He groaned, lifted his eyes to the sky in a demoralised kind of way, and went back inside the caravan.

Aidan was still shaking his head as they drove away. 'Will you stop doing that, please?' Daisy barked at him.

'If you stop playing the hapless old biddie.'

She let out a silly giggle. 'So would you have preferred I let them see the real me, and become a murder suspect in the process?'

He shook his head for the last time. 'Perhaps not. I might have emphasised my advancing years a little, while that bundle of joy called DCI Burrows was interviewing me.'

'Well then, you're just as bad as me.' She caught the look. 'Ok then, just not as good an actor.'

'Is that a compliment?'

'You decide. And step on the gas. We've got a torn-up note to piece together.'

Daisy laid out the eight jigsaw pieces on the counter top of the island unit, and put on her reading glasses to try and see what was written there. Aidan placed a cup of nuclear-level coffee next to her, and put an arm around her as he strained to see the words.

59

'There's not much there,' he said quietly.

'No, and it doesn't seem to make any sense either. Hand me the cellotape, I need to fix them together properly.'

She worked away for a minute or two, intricately taping the pieces together at the back. Then she turned the paper round, and together they looked at what was written there...

WL27/rb/fg/cntr/pnk.f

Daisy glanced up to Aidan. 'This is obviously significant, and it's some kind of code. Maybe for a computer?'

This time he shook his head. 'Doesn't look like a computer code. Quite frankly it's not like anything I've come across before.'

'Come on, dear. You used to be an accountant. You must have had all kinds of secret codes when you were cooking books. Just get your brain into gear.'

'I'll ignore that remark. I never cooked books... well, as far as the taxman was concerned anyway. Tell you what... this is going to take some time to figure out. Make me another smoothie, and while you do that I'll get my galactic-sized brain around it and see what I can decipher. Deal?'

'Deal.'

'I think it's a collection note.'

Daisy clunked the smoothie glass onto the island unit top, to help fuel Aidan's galactic-sized brain. 'Collection note?'

'Of sorts. Look... Matilda lives at number twenty-seven. WL27.'

'The postcode... kind of. WL... Walcotts Lane. But what does the rest mean?' She picked up the note, studied it for a few seconds, and nodded her head.

'Yes.'

'Yes?'

'Yes... once you know what WL27 stands for, the rest falls into place.'

'It does?'

'Come on, dear. I know even you aren't that thick.'

'I beg your pardon?'

She tapped him on the shoulder. 'I guess you just wanted me to solve it first.'

'Maybe.'

'There's no need to be so chivalrous, and you hardly need to be a rocket scientist. Rb means rose bush; fg stands for front garden; cntr is short for centre.'

'Genius at work. But what does pnk.f stand for?'

You never were much of a gardener, were you dear?'

He frowned, and then smiled. 'Ah.'

'I'm assuming neither was the dealer who tried to collect it, which is why Jesse wanted to make absolutely sure he knew it was a rose with pink flowers.'

'Hmm... so this note isn't really much use to us. Jesse wanted to distance himself from the people he was supplying. He texts the dealer the code, who writes it down on a piece of paper and then goes to collect in the middle of the night. They never meet.'

'But that guy knew where Jesse lived, and probably made sure he did. As a kind of insurance, so if anything went wrong, like two old fogies getting to the package first, he could go have it out with him.'

61

'And Jesse had already kept his side of the deal, so didn't have the package, but had no way to prove he hadn't done the dirty on him.'

'Which resulted in some kind of altercation, which then led to the dealer getting angry, tearing up the code he'd scribbled down, throwing the slivers of paper over Jesse, and then stabbing him.'

'Which given the huge sum of money involved, was probably understandable.' Daisy dabbed away a tear, the nagging voice in her head telling her if she'd just thought harder about it, they should have left the package where it was.

Aidan stood up, pulled her into him and gave her a hug. 'Hindsight is a dangerous thing, Daisy. It tends to scream at people and tell them they've done the wrong thing, but only after the event. And before the event, neither of us knew what we do now.'

'I know, dear,' she whispered into his shoulder. 'But it doesn't stop me feeling guilty for being an interfering old codger.'

Chapter 12

It was almost four in the afternoon when the front door was almost hammered off its cast-iron hinges.

Daisy and Aidan had spent a couple of hours trying to work out what their next move was. The torn-up note seemed like it might have been a lead to finding the bad guys, but they'd had to admit it was simply a collection note. It had given them more insight to what must have happened in Jesse's caravan, but was no real value in helping to progress their unofficial investigation any further.

Not in the best of moods, the thunderous noise at the front door set Daisy's nerve-ends tingling, and not in a good way. She stomped half-angrily to the door, and wrenched it open.

'Oh, it's you.'

'Yes, it's me. So what have you got to say for yourself?'

'Are you going to pay to fix the knuckle-dents in my door?'

That stopped the breathing of fire in mid-flame. 'What?'

'You heard. Or do I send the parish council the bill?'

'What?'

'Look... there's a bit of scorched paint too. I'll have to repaint the whole door now.'

Matilda couldn't help glancing at the door, even though she knew it was perfectly fine. 'I don't appreciate your peculiar sense of humour, Daisy Morrow. Or the inference, come to that,' she flamed out huffily.

'What do you want, Matilda?'

'I want to know if you are aware of what you've done.'

'Me?'

'Yes, you. I've just left about a hundred police officers digging up my front garden...'

'I doubt there's a hundred, Matilda.'

'That's not the point. The point is, my garden resembles a building site, and I've been interrogated like a criminal. All the neighbours are staring at me, and it's utterly embarrassing. And it's all your fault.'

'Mine? Did they not tell you it's part of a murder investigation, Matilda? And that it's Jesse who's dead?'

'Of course they did. That miserable so-and-so of an inspector filled me in... and told me it was you who'd trespassed in my garden in the middle of the night. So what have you got to say for yourself?'

'Did he tell you what we found in your garden?'

'Well... no. He just said a serious crime had been committed. And then I got the bright light treatment, while he accused me of having something to do with it.'

'Did you have something to do with it?'

Matilda did a full, less-than-dainty pirouette of frustration, and then threw her arms in the air. 'Of course I didn't. I'm an important member of the parish council, as you well know.'

Daisy sighed, and tried to find a way to bring the baptism of fire to an end. 'Matilda, I'm sorry you got involved. DCI Burrows was just doing his job, making sure you weren't involved rather than trying to prove you were. I'm sure he doesn't think a... law-abiding, fine upstanding person like you would ever be involved in such serious crimes.'

'Crimes?' she shrieked. 'You mean there's more than one?'

'Matilda, go back and talk with the inspector. Regardless of what he was up to, our village gardener is dead. That is a tragedy in itself, so please have some respect for that.'

'Respect? He's soiled everything... literally. My beautiful village will never be the same again. And now I'll have to find someone else to fix my garden.'

Aidan appeared over Daisy's shoulder, and glanced deliberately at the door. 'Oh dear, those scorch marks will have to be repainted, dear,' he said.

Matilda huffed mightily, but then, like a dragon all out of flames, stomped away across the drive, chuntering loudly as she went. 'I should have known better than to get any sympathy out of you two. And I will be sending you the bill...'

'Thank god she's gone,' Aidan let out a sigh of relief as the fire-breathing dragon disappeared from sight.

'Yes, but she does have a point. Her rose bush was literally in the right place at the wrong time, and now she's paying the price. I very much doubt the police will leave things exactly as they found them.'

'I guess so. But it was hardly our fault. Even if we'd left the package where it was, ultimately she'd still have ended up being put through the mill when we were forced to tell the police the truth.'

Daisy flicked on the kettle, feeling the need for a nice cup of tea to settle her unease. 'You're right of course, dear. But it's all very unfortunate. And destiny chose the worst person it could to deal its hand to. It'll be all over the notice board and the parish newsletter that we're the bad guys. The next thing you know, we'll be the ones who murdered Jesse.'

He gave her a hug. 'Let's just have a cup of tea, and chill out a bit.'

Daisy smiled a very unconvincing smile as she poured water onto two teabags. 'I do need to find out something

65

though... whether the police found anything in Jesse's caravan after we left.'

Neither of them knew it right then, but three hours later Daisy was to get an answer to that question. And although she'd always known she would get another visit from the police, the person who actually turned up, and how she was dressed, was somewhat more unexpected.

Chapter 13

It was just gone seven in the evening when the front door knocked again. Daisy and Aidan had spent a couple of hours bouncing a few pertinent facts off each other, but had to admit without more information from the police, which was hardly likely to be forthcoming, there wasn't much more they could think. Little did they know, someone was about to walk through the door who could give them that information.

It wasn't the Thor's-hammer-type thunderous thumping of three hours previously. More the gentle knock of someone who held a lot more respect for elderly people.

Daisy glanced to Aidan, busy creating a culinary masterpiece on the hob. 'Who can that be, at this time of the evening?'

'Well, it isn't the fire-breathing dragon again. The door's still on its hinges.'

She headed to the front door, and as she opened it, her face broke into a beaming smile.

'Sarah!'

The young policewoman smiled an uncertain smile back. 'I'm so sorry to disturb you, Mrs. Morrow. I just have a couple of questions for you, if I can steal a few minutes of your time? Is it too late for you?'

Daisy switched instantly into a slight stoop. 'Not at all. We were just about to eat. Would you like to join us?'

'Oh, I... I couldn't impose.'

'Trust me, dear, it's no imposition. Aidan always makes enough to feed a small army. And I make good use of my freezer!' She shuffled aside. 'Please, come in.'

Daisy looked the young woman over, a slight frown on her brow she did her best to hide. The pristine uniform was gone, replaced by a smart pair of dark-blue jeans, and a white collared blouse with a pale-blue tailored jacket over the top.

The tight bun and silly female police hat was gone too, her silky blonde hair allowed to tumble just below her slender shoulders. She wasn't exactly dressed for formal police business. And looking like she did, she reminded Daisy even more of someone she once knew.

Aidan gave her a warm smile as they walked into the kitchen. 'You must have smelled my gourmet chilli con carne, Sarah. It is irresistible after all.'

'Oh, no... I didn't realise...'

He grinned. 'Glass of wine?'

'Um... I don't think I should, on duty.'

Daisy gave her a knowing smile. 'You don't exactly look like you're on duty, Constable Sarah Lowry.'

She glanced down at her smart-casual attire. 'Well... the uniform puts people off sometimes.'

'Is that the only reason?'

'Maybe not. Perhaps... perhaps this isn't official police business.'

Aidan pressed a large glass of Pinot Noir in her hand. 'Red ok?'

She nodded, in the kind of way that told them both she'd been sussed. But she still tried to justify being there. 'I do have a couple of questions, though... kind of official.'

Daisy indicated a chair next to the small table, as Aidan placed three warmed plates onto it. 'Kind of official?'

'Well... my boss wants to quiz you both tomorrow, and he's... a little brusque sometimes. I thought if I asked you more informally tonight, it wouldn't be too much for you to cope with if he gets his teeth into you.'

Daisy smiled. 'Oh my dear, that's so thoughtful of you. Even if I don't believe you for a moment.'

Aidan threw her a curious glance as he piled the chilli and rice onto the three plates. He knew just as well as Daisy did the subterfuge of playing the senior citizens had suddenly flown right out of the window. And he knew why.

Sarah's pretty face blushed a shade to match the red roses growing up against the front window. 'I suppose my suspicions are confirmed then.'

Daisy narrowed her eyes. 'So is this in any way official?'

'I suppose not really.'

'Be more positive, dear.'

'No. No it isn't. But the bit about my boss intending to quiz you tomorrow is true.'

'So your motives for coming are honourable, if somewhat disguised?'

Sarah looked up and smiled at the words. 'Yes, that's a good evaluation.'

'So, are you going to undisguise them?'

She took a mouthful of the chilli. 'Oh, this is delicious. Thank you, Aidan.'

Daisy narrowed her eyes. 'Stop trying to avoid the question. We're not the dozy old cronies we made out earlier, which you were clearly perceptive enough to realise.'

Her eyes dropped to the tabletop, and a slightly-shaky hand reached out for the wineglass. 'That's... that's kind of why I came.'

Daisy put a hand on her arm. 'Sarah, relax. Just tell us what's on that clever mind of yours.'

69

She sank a big swig of the wine, and nodded. 'That... act might have fooled my boss, because that's what he expected to find with you two. But if you think about it logically, it didn't really make sense.'

'Senior citizens often don't make sense, dear,' said Daisy deliberately.

'Ok, you can stop it now,' Sarah grinned. 'It didn't seem to make any sense... two elderly residents, one with a mobility scooter, having the intelligence to suspect Jesse was up to something, raiding a neighbour's garden in the middle of the night to find out what he's up to, and then going to confront him about it the next morning? It sounds like something you'd find on Tales of the Unexpected.'

Aidan shook his head and grinned. 'I'm not sure I like the inference. They're all weirdoes on that show.'

Sarah laughed, the wine doing its intended job and helping to relax her. 'Sorry. But you know what I mean.'

Daisy was frowning. 'So do you now suspect anything else?'

'Oh, no... I'm not saying you're murder suspects or anything like that.'

'Thank god for that.'

Aidan threw Daisy a glance, but then flicked his gaze to Sarah. 'So did your suspicions about us go any further?'

Suddenly she looked really uncomfortable. 'I'm sorry... I am a policewoman after all.'

Daisy nodded. 'And police officers use all the technology available to them these days to look into people.'

'They... we do. But I didn't tell anyone else I was looking into you. I promise.'

'Let me be clear... no one else at Lynn police has any idea what line of investigation you were pursuing?'

She nodded, in a slightly embarrassed way. 'No one. I don't exactly know why, but I kept it to myself. And also, I kept what I discovered to myself.'

'And what did you discover?'

'I discovered that both of you moved here from London a year ago. But before that, neither of you seemed to exist.'

Chapter 14

'There is a reason for that.'

Aidan threw a don't-say-too-much glance to Daisy, but she knew she had to say something.

'Our records were officially wiped from the system because of my previous employment. And because, three years ago, something tragic happened, which eventually led to us moving here, hopefully to enjoy our retirement in some kind of peace. A rather vain hope, it seems.'

'Oh gosh... I'm so sorry. But... ordinary people can't just have their records sponged.'

'We're not ordinary people, dear. Well, Aidan is... he's just an accountant.'

'Just..?'

Daisy tapped him affectionately on the arm. 'Let's just say my former bosses made it happen, and leave it at that, shall we?'

'Oh I say... how exciting!'

'Well, once upon a time it was, but when you get to my age dear, with my old bones...'

'I said you can stop it now, Daisy.'

She grinned, and refilled Sarah's glass. 'Sorry... new habits die hard too, you know.'

Something occurred to Aidan, which furrowed deep lines into his brow. 'I need to ask you, Sarah... in light of the fact we've now confirmed your very insightful suspicions, what do you intend to do with that knowledge, you being a rookie policewoman and all that?'

'Oh, I don't know. I hadn't thought that far.'

Daisy smiled, already knowing their secret was safe. 'Even though you came to visit us in your civvies?'

Again she looked down to her lap, a little embarrassed. 'I suppose I wanted to confirm my thoughts first, and then decide what to do. I'm sorry.'

Daisy wrapped a hand around Sarah's. 'Don't be sorry. You'd already been clever enough to work out we were putting on an act, and you did so before your technology, and now us, confirmed it. I admire you for that. But now I have to ask you something, as an ex-civil servant to a brand new one.'

She nodded. 'Keep what I found to myself.'

Daisy smiled to confirm her answer. 'What made you join the police in the first place, dear?'

'My father was a cop, recently taken early retirement... and I suppose we both wanted me to carry on from where he left off, and fight the bad guys on behalf of the good guys.'

'And do you believe being in the police force is the only way to do that?'

'I guess you're going to tell me otherwise?'

'Let's just say that sometimes, the official Brit response tends to lack that sharp edge. I am a great admirer of the police, my dear, but in some ways their effectiveness is constrained by law. Which might sound a contradiction in terms.'

'It does rather.'

'Back in the day, the Metropolitan Police Force was a great ally, but also a hindrance. I discovered the hard way that sometimes being above the law was a great freedom to have. Sadly, the same can be said about hardened criminals, who think the same way but for entirely different reasons. I became convinced that in some things, going it alone can have a... more satisfying outcome, shall we say.'

'Oh wow... I want to be you!'

Daisy put on a stern face. 'Now don't get carried away, Sarah. Being me had its consequences, and not exactly good ones. But having said that... and please switch off the recording, dear...'

Sarah knew exactly what Daisy was saying. 'It's ok. We're not in Interview Room One, and I'm not on duty.'

'Having said that... if you can accept that our wonderful police force has its limitations, you could be of great help to us.'

'Oh I say... you want me to be a double-agent?'

Daisy grinned. 'Well, maybe wear two hats, metaphorically speaking. Aidan and I are determined to find the bad guys, but we've come to a bit of a dead end with clues. So we need someone on the inside, to keep us abreast of developments. I know it's a lot to ask, dear.'

'Yes, it is. In one way.'

'One way?'

Sarah nodded. 'In the strict letter of the law, if I divulge police information I could be fired, if anyone found out.'

'That's why it's a lot to ask.'

'But in another way... it's so exciting!'

'So which way wins out?'

'I have a condition.'

'Go on.'

'I'll be your eyes in the Kings Lynn police, if you rope me in to your unofficial activities.'

Aidan frowned again. 'We're not private detectives, Sarah.'

'Aren't you?'

Daisy butted in. 'Oh, of course we are. And we would be delighted for you to join us in an unofficial capacity, dear. So, let's start by you telling us what you've found out so far. Chocolate cheesecake?'

As they devoured dessert, Daisy pumped Sarah for everything she knew. It wasn't much, but it gave them a few pertinent facts they didn't have before.

'There were no prints anywhere other than Jesse's.'

'The murderer wore gloves. No surprise there.'

'And we couldn't find the knife, or a phone. Whoever did it took it with him.'

'That's hardly surprising either. Jesse's phone would likely be incriminating.'

'We did find eight and a half thousand pounds though, stashed in a tin at the back of a cupboard.'

'The spoils of illegal activities.' Aidan shook his head again.

'But did you find any more packages?'

She shook her head. 'No. Forensics even dug up his garden, seeing as he was a gardener and all, but there was nothing.'

Daisy narrowed her eyes. 'Somehow I doubt he'd keep his stash in the caravan, or his garden. From what we can gather so far, he kept his little sideline well private from the rest of his life. Remote collections in someone else's garden, it was almost like he was keeping it anonymous.'

'Not anonymous enough though,' Aidan was still shaking his head.

Daisy laughed humourlessly. 'When you're part of a major drugs gang, Mister Big will always make sure he's got an insurance policy for if things go wrong.'

'Like a couple of old cronies sticking a spanner in the works.'

'Don't remind me. But I don't think he'd keep his stash far from home. The police didn't find it, but I guarantee it's around somewhere.'

Sarah looked excited again. 'So you think we should look for it?'

'Perhaps. But let's not get carried away. First off there's the little problem of Burrows discovering Aidan and me are not what he thought.'

'I think I can help there. He asked me to look into everyone who might or might not have been involved. When I go in tomorrow I can tell him you two are just a couple of nosy old parkers, and persuade him interviewing you is a waste of time.'

'Even though you know different?' said Aidan.

Daisy shot him down. 'Dear, don't be such a dipstick. Sarah is one of us now. She just has to make sure she convinces the powers-that-be that we're harmless and helpless!'

'Don't worry. I can do it!'

'But do you want to?'

'Oh yes. Private crime-solving is much more fascinating than police work.'

'I might hold you to that.'

'Hope you do. But I'd better now go. It's getting late.'

'Do you live far away?'

'East Winch. I've got the annex at my parents' home.'

Aidan grabbed his phone. 'Another village. You can't drive home, you've had too much Pinot to accompany the baring of souls. I'll call you a taxi, and you can pick your car up tomorrow, and tell us how pulling the wool over Burrows' eyes went.'

Daisy and Aidan waved the taxi away, and then he closed the gate and followed her back inside.

'Well, that was an event,' said Daisy.

'It surely was.'

76

'I hear a 'but' in your tone.'

'The but is that I hope by the cold light of day, Sarah doesn't get spooked and tell all.'

'Oh ye of little faith. She said she wouldn't, so she won't.'

He threw his coat around his shoulders. 'You seem to have more faith than I do. And I know what's prompting that faith.'

'No fooling you, dear.'

They walked together to the kitchen door. 'I've not been through the ups and downs of the last few years by your side without knowing you better than anyone. And the resemblance is quite strong.'

She gave him a hug, holding onto him a little longer than usual. 'It's not just a physical resemblance though, is it? There's so many ways...'

He kissed her gently. 'Just be sure the memories don't cloud the reality, darling. This is a whole new ball game, and so is Sarah.'

'I won't, dear. Tempting though it is.'

She watched him as he crossed the drive and disappeared from view. Then she turned back to the door, and wiped away a tear. She knew why he'd warned her as gently as he had, and she knew all too well that their new ally was bringing back both painful and joyful memories.

The man she'd spent the last thirty-five years with was looking out for her emotional wellbeing. He'd obviously seen the same resemblance, felt the same surge of memories she had. And he knew how dangerous it was to let those things get in the way of sound reasoning.

A total stranger had brought with her a strange glow of familiarity. It gave Daisy a good feeling. No, Sarah wasn't Celia. But she could have been the sister Celia never had.

Chapter 15

Constable Sarah Lowry made sure she was in the squad room at Kings Lynn police station before her boss arrived. In truth, she made the station so early she was the only one there, apart from a couple of people on night duty, just about to end their shift.

It gave her time to grab a coffee, and sink down behind her desk to find a little peace before everyone else arrived for their day's work. It also gave her time to think. Which might not have been the best thing.

After she'd got home from Daisy's the previous night, and settled in the annex of her parents' home, it had almost been time for sleep. After a tiring day with her boss, examining Jesse's caravan for clues to his murderer, which were sadly lacking, and then a hasty couple of hours poring over the station PC, had taken its toll on her energy levels. That had been followed by the illogical need to visit Daisy and Aidan to confess about the discoveries she'd made, which certainly didn't help.

It had been a long day, both physically and emotionally. Daisy's acceptance of the fact she'd delved into her past had been followed by her own equally-illogical need to become a part of their unofficial quest to find out more.

She couldn't quite understand herself, but the need for sleep had overtaken the desire to self-examine. Yet now, in the cold light of day, and in the stark reality of the squad room, the enormity of what she was doing smacked her right in the face.

She told herself the police department didn't have strict rules and regulations about what officers did in their spare time. It wasn't helping much. Working with Daisy as a 'hobby' in her down time was one thing, but she knew just as well as she did that in order to do that, she would have to divulge things those outside the police force should by rights never be privy to.

That wasn't sitting easily. Everything she'd been brought up to believe by her father, and everything she'd taken on board in her training and in the six months she'd actually been a fully-fledged constable, was telling her police business should stay police business.

But she'd also seen the limitations of that police force, and Daisy's words had struck a raw kind of nerve. Her boss was seriously experienced, and she could learn a lot from him. But over the years he'd become jaded by the murky world he spent much of his time existing in. He saw things the way 'old-school' inspectors saw them, and was old enough to never intend changing that mindset.

He even disapproved of female officers, believing police work was man's domain. It was only the new rules that obliged him to take her on at all, and the fact she was a 'new-school' constable meant they clashed on occasions. But he was her boss, and as a rookie, she had little choice but to succumb to his orders.

Constable Sarah Lowry saw being a cop as her duty. But somewhere deep inside, it didn't excite her as much as being a part of Daisy's world.

And despite the misgivings that prodded a very sharp knife into her sensible side, she couldn't ignore the appeal of the unexpected that seemed to surround her new friend.

Despite the trouble it might bring them, and everyone around them.

She smiled an excited kind of smile, and made up her mind. Being a part of Daisy's investigation might be against the official rules, but it wouldn't have to matter.

She and Aidan needed protecting from themselves, and from the danger they might fall into. Constable Sarah Lowry had decided she was the one to provide it.

'Anything interesting on our victims... or whatever else they might be?'

She looked up from the screen as Burrows ambled into the squad room an hour later. He smelt of cigarettes, and had his big hand wrapped around a mug of nuclear-level coffee.

'No sir... Matilda Ogden and Maisie Williams were indeed victims, as clean as a whistle. Just in the wrong place at the wrong time. Or at least, their gardens were. Daisy Morrow and Aidan Henderson were just nosy old cronies, who happened to stumble on the package. Luckily for us.'

'Hmm... let's hope we've seen the end of their doddery old nosing around. There's something worrying about them, as far as my gut is concerned at least. Like they were putting on some kind of act for our benefit.'

'Oh, I think they're well-meaning but helpless, sir. And even if they did want to nose further, there's really no way for them to interfere.' She apologised silently to her father, who was very likely frowning metaphorically at her deliberate lies. 'What about forensics? Did they find anything?'

He sank his butt wearily onto the end of the desk, even though it was just the start of the day. 'Not a ruddy thing. Nothing to give us a clue, and no more so-called bags of flour. They dug up the whole garden too. However... luckily that side of things won't be our concern later today.'

'Sir?'

'Given the quantity we found...'

'The quantity Daisy and Aidan found, sir,' Sarah corrected.

'Hmph. Yes, if you like. But given the quantity, the Drugs Squad is taking over that side of things. They'll be here in a few hours. It's a pretty safe bet we've only discovered the tip of the iceberg so far. It'll still be our responsibility to try and find the killer, but given the lack of clues, that won't be easy.'

'Is there a team doing house-to-house... well, caravan to-caravan, sir?'

'Yes, and I guess we'd better go and join them. Not that it'll get us very far; half the residents there have some kind of criminal record, so they're going to clam up like raw oysters.'

Sarah closed the PC, and followed her boss to his car. He was all too right; today's knocking on doors wouldn't get them anywhere. But for the time being it was all they could do officially. She shook her head, resigning herself to the mundane hours of fruitless questions ahead, but knowing that later on, when she went to collect her car, she could at least tell her new friends she'd kept their secret safe.

But there was something she'd not revealed to them. She still wasn't sure if she should. When she'd been delving into Daisy's past, she'd gone further back than she'd let on.

Hers and Aidan's records had been purged, at the request of whoever it was she worked for in her past life. But they'd not been able to purge the births, marriages and death's register. It had taken some digging, but she'd finally discovered that Daisy and Aidan were a lot more than just good friends.

Chapter 16

Aidan appeared in Daisy's kitchen just after ten. She poured him a coffee, and then they spent a couple of hours doing nothing that really needed doing. Just gone midday, Daisy's itchy feet got the better of her, although it was perhaps nearer the truth that everything was itching, and refusing to be scratched better.

'Let's go to Maisie's, see if she needs any moral support,' she said, in a flustered kind of way.

Aidan grinned. 'Two hours of inactivity, and your blood pressure is already at boiling point?'

'I just need to do something. Take my mind off Sarah popping in later.'

'I thought you had faith?'

'I do. But sometimes faith can be misplaced.'

As soon as they made the pavement and caught sight of Maisie's front garden, they both shook their heads. She was there, furiously working away with a trowel, desperately trying to put her pride and joy back together after the police had virtually dug everything up.

There were tears in her eyes as she glanced up and saw them approaching. 'Look at it,' she said in a shaky voice. 'All my years of work, ruined.'

Daisy glanced guiltily to Aidan. To be fair the police had tried their best to be as respectful as possible, but in the short space of time they'd had, the garden was never going to be left to Maisie's liking. But she couldn't be abandoned to deal with the aftermath alone... especially as Daisy and Aidan were the people who'd ultimately caused it.

Daisy grabbed the spade leaning up against the bungalow wall. 'Maisie, go make us a cup of tea. Aidan and me will help.'

Three hours later the garden was at least looking more Maisie-like. It would take a few weeks of growing time to hide all the scars, but at least its owner looked a little happier. She thanked them both, but as they walked the short distance to Aidan's bungalow, Daisy couldn't keep the scowl from her face.

'I have to do something. Something real,' she growled.

'Like what?'

'Go for a drive.'

He knew straightaway what their ultimate destination would be. 'Daisy, that's not a good idea... there'll still be police around, it's too soon.'

'Maybe, but it might give me a light bulb moment of inspiration.'

'Why don't we just wait until Sarah comes round?'

'That's probably at least three hours away. What am I supposed to do until then?'

'The vacuuming?'

'Don't be absurd.'

Aidan lifted his hands from his sides, a tried and tested indication that he knew it was pointless arguing. Visiting the trailer park so soon was a bad idea, but for Daisy's itchy everything it was the best idea ever. He grabbed the keys from the dining table, and three minutes later they were approaching the entrance to the park.

As soon as they turned into the narrow asphalt lanes they could see how things had changed. The only indication of human life was the occasional flash of a police visi-jacket.

The residents had not only clammed up their gobs, they'd clammed up their lives as well.

'I guess it was to be expected. Half of them will just pretend they're not in, the other half won't have seen a single thing out of the ordinary.'

'I doubt there was much to see anyway. Most of them were probably asleep when it happened.'

'Just a drive-past, ok Daisy? If we stop now with all these police around, it'll look suspicious.'

She sighed. 'Yes, I know dear.'

They didn't get as far as Jesse's van. Just as they passed next to one of the permanent park homes, the door opened and someone they knew looked at them with a horrified expression on her face. Aidan eased the car to a stop.

'What the hell are you doing here?' hissed Sarah, glancing around furtively.

'Blame Daisy's itchy everything,' said Aidan.

'Well, just go... now. Burrows is here somewhere, and if he sees you there'll be awkward questions to answer. He's already got a gut feeling you're acting out an episode of The Archers. Just get out of here.'

'Nice to see you too,' said Daisy huffily.

'She's right, dear.'

'Don't you start.'

'I am right. So get lost.'

'Well, I know when I'm not wanted.'

'Good. I'll see you later, ok?'

'Kids.'

'I'm not a kid.'

'Just button it, dear. Pretend you're a responsible person.'

'Stuff you.'

'Please just go.'

Aidan shoved his foot on the throttle, and the car moved away before Daisy could utter any more expletives.

'Well I didn't know Burrows would be there, did I?'

'No, of course you didn't, dear.'

'Don't be so patronising.'

'So what was that all about?'

Daisy caught the look, and the glare, on Constable Sarah Lowry's face. 'Just out for an afternoon drive, dear,' she smiled sweetly.

'You can't fool me, you nosy old biddie.'

Daisy, leading the way into the kitchen and grabbing the kettle, stared at her in shocked silence. For a moment the world went to freeze-frame, and then the two of them burst into fits of giggles.

'I suppose I am a nosy old biddie,' Daisy wiped the tears of laughter from her eyes.

'Yes, you are. Just don't try anything that idiotic again. If Burrows had seen you, his gut feeling would probably have turned into an arrest warrant, and then all your secrets would be out.'

'I'm suitably chastised.'

'Good. Just don't let your impatient side bring you any more trouble.'

'I'm just going to Aidan's for dinner. You want to join us?'

'Oh, no I can't really. Just collecting my car. Dad's got dinner brewing, and after yesterday I need an early night. Thanks all the same.'

Daisy gave her a disappointed pout. 'Shame. So is there anything you can tell me?'

'Not so far, just that I think I can keep Burrows off your back, if you don't pull any more idiotic stunts. The drugs

85

squad have taken over the bag-of-flour side of things, but we're still handling the murder investigation. Not that it's really going anywhere right now.'

Daisy laughed ironically. 'Village people have a habit of clamming up when their little world is disturbed. It's ten times worse when that disturbance takes place on a caravan park semi-populated by people who feel stigmatised by the law. Best of luck with that.'

Sarah headed to the door, and then held something out. 'Here Daisy, that's my official card. I've written my mobile number on the back, so we can keep in touch... unofficially. And... can I ask you something?'

'Of course.'

'Why don't you and Aidan live together?'

'That's a strange question, dear. We're just friends. Why do you ask?'

'Oh... um... just that you two are so close. It seemed logical, somehow.'

Daisy patted her on the shoulder. 'In our generation, dear, living together is somewhat frowned upon. What would Matilda think?'

Sarah gave a tiny shake of the head as she headed to her car, but it was enough for Daisy's eagle-eyes to notice. As she closed the gate and headed to Aidan's, she couldn't shift the odd feeling her new friend knew a little more than she was letting on.

Chapter 17

Just before nine, Aidan walked Daisy back through the alley to the cottage. Once again it was almost dark, but not quite. They made the front gate, and he glanced to the house and frowned.

'You didn't leave a light on, Daisy,' he said.

'I thought I had. But then again, my mind was full of Sarah's words, and we walked out together. I just forgot.'

He squeezed her hand. 'Sleep well, darling. I'll be here in the morning, to make you breakfast.'

She hugged him tightly, and watched as he disappeared from view back into the alley.

The reassuring light of the porch lamps flicked on as they detected her movement, and cast their warm glow across the gravel drive as she made her way to the side door, closed it behind her, and switched on the kitchen light.

It didn't come on. For a moment a wave of nervousness wafted through her. The big space of the combined kitchen and daytime living area was in virtual darkness, and for a second it made her uneasy. Then she shook her head sheepishly at the unexpected nerves that were playing tricks with her. Bulbs failed all the time, it was nothing to get spooked about.

She ambled over to where the switch behind the cupboard trims would turn on the wall cupboard lights. A mellow light flooded the room.

But her finger hadn't reached the light switch.

She spun round. The table lamps in the sitting area had come on, all by themselves.

Not all by themselves.

Someone was sitting in the armchair. Someone very tall and gangly, his long legs splayed out before him, and a confident, menacing grin on his face.

Someone who wasn't supposed to be there.

'Bout friggin' time. Been waiting here for hours.'

Daisy pulled herself together. It wasn't the first time she'd found someone in her house who wasn't supposed to be there, after all. But it had been quite a while, and certainly not in Norfolk. She tried to keep the nervous shake from her voice.

'I doubt it's been hours. People like you don't break into houses in broad daylight.'

'Geez, lady. That's a bit presumptuous.'

She switched on a smile, mostly to hide the shock, walked closer to the grinning intruder and looked him over. He was still spread-eagled in the armchair, but appeared to be about eight feet tall. Black jeans and a leather jacket covered a thin slender body, and a black face with even darker sunglasses was topped off with a colourful Rasta hat.

'You're in my favourite chair.'

'Hell, girl. You got balls, I'll give you that. You find a scary dude in your place, and all you can say is he's in your favourite chair?'

'Are you scary? You don't look very scary to me.'

'I's scary, trust me.'

'We'll see about that. Cup of tea?'

'What?'

Daisy walked back to the kitchen area, her trained eyes watching out of their corners for any sudden movement from the intruder. She needn't have worried. Stunned by her apparently flippant attitude, he seemed to be frozen to his spread-eagled spot, an inane, open-mouthed expression on his face.

'Milk and sugar?' she asked as she flicked on the kettle, starting to realise her visitor wasn't quite as scary as he was making out to be.

'What's your name, son?'

'What?'

'Can't you say any other words? What's your name?'

He finally closed his mouth, but opened it again to say other words. 'It's Des. Well, Desmond, but that makes me sound like an old Jamaican hairdresser.'

'You're not old enough to know about ancient TV sitcoms.'

'Hey, I watch Channel Four.'

'So, tell me what a Jamaican youth is doing sitting in my favourite armchair.'

He looked a little disgruntled. 'I ain't a youth. And how d'ya know I's Jamaican?'

'The green, yellow and red beanie hat kinda gives it away.'

'Oh... yeah. I see now.'

'Amazed you can see anything in those idiotic sunglasses. It's night, unless you can't see that either.'

'You diggin' at me?' he said in a high-pitched voice, deciding to take off the sunglasses anyway.

Daisy put a mug of tea on the little table next to the chair. 'Of course not. So what can I do for you, son?'

'Stop calling me that. I ain't your son. And I's here to scare the living shit outa yous.'

'I see.' Daisy sipped her mug of tea, making sure she was at a safe distance, and staying on her feet. 'Have you actually done this kind of thing before?'

He looked a little flustered by the inference. 'Hey lady. It's supposed to be me aksin' the questions.'

'Oh please, Desmond. Aks away.'

'It's Des.'

'My mistake.'

'You's taking to piss outa me?'

'Would I?'

'You's don't seem very terrified of me.'

'Oh, I'm quaking in my boots, believe me.'

It was said with a heavy dose of sarcasm, and as soon as her gob had uttered the words, Daisy knew it might have pushed her visitor a step too far. She wasn't wrong. Ordered to the cottage to achieve a couple of objectives, he was starting to realise both were proving harder than he'd thought.

He pulled a knife out of his jacket pocket, and waved it around menacingly, his face clouded into the kind of expression a cornered deer would exhibit.

'Geez, does this get you quaking in your boots, old lady?'

Daisy checked up. Her acid tongue had pushed him close to the edge. His boss, whoever he was, had clearly sent him on a mission where failure wasn't an option. He was just as scared as she suddenly was. Going back and reporting an epic fail was something he wasn't going to fancy in the slightest. A scenario that meant the next couple of minutes were going to be as unpredictable as him.

She was defenceless. And somehow that wasn't a good thing.

She deliberately bent over a little. 'Oh... oh dear...'

'What?' He was leaning forward in the chair, pointing the knife at her in a shaky hand.

'Dear, I'm so sorry... I needed the loo when I came in, and now you're pointing that... thing at me, well... it's suddenly got desperate. Please may I use the bathroom?'

He shook his head, not quite believing the words he was hearing. 'Just... just hold it, lady.'

'I can't, dear. Oh, it's coming...'

'Geez, what is it with you geriatrics? Ok, but I'm coming with you.'

'Excuse me? I'm a frail old lady, son. I do require a modicum of privacy, you know.'

He spun his eyes to the left and then the right, like that would give him the answer to his prayers. 'Oh hell. Where's the bathroom?'

Daisy pointed a deliberately shaky hand to the walkway next to the island unit. 'The downstairs bathroom is just there. You can see the door from here... please?'

He stood up, his head almost touching the low ceiling, and waved the knife in the direction of the passageway. 'Ok. Just be quick. We got business to attend to.'

'Oh... oh dear... I have no option but to be quick.'

Daisy hurried to the bathroom, making sure she did so while still a little bent over. She closed and locked the door, and was as noisy as possible lifting the toilet lid.

She had to move fast. Desmond wasn't going to wait very long before he came knocking. She didn't fancy a 'here's Johnny' scenario. She flushed the toilet, and turned on the basin tap so hopefully he'd think she was washing her hands. Then she headed quickly for the door.

But not the one back to the passageway. The small room next to the bathroom had a connecting door to it. The previous occupants had used it as a bedroom, and the bathroom doubled up as a kind of en suite. When Daisy moved in, the room next door became her office. She'd intended blocking the connecting door off at some point, but as she stepped into the office, she breathed a sigh of relief she'd not yet got round to it.

There was something there she really needed.

She wrenched open the door to the cabinet that most offices don't have, and grabbed a weapon. There was no time to load it, but her visitor wouldn't know that. She slipped back into the bathroom, and unlocked the door to the passageway.

'Whoa... you crazy, bitch?'

Desmond, six feet from the entrance to the passageway, backed off in shock. It was maybe understandable. A crazed pensioner brandishing an AK-47 in his direction was surely the last thing he expected to see.

'Geez, dude... you got a licence for that thing?'

'Sure I have... you think I break the law, punk?' said Daisy in her best Clint Eastwood, omitting the fact she had a licence for a lot more. And deciding not to tell him it had expired over ten years ago. 'Now... now it's time to get down to business.'

Desmond's big eyes glanced at the rather small knife in his hand, and then at the ceiling as he shook his head. 'Aw Momma... it's supposed to be me sayin' that.'

Daisy ratcheted back the charging handle of the automatic rifle, ready to fire. 'Why are you here, Desmond?'

'It's Des. Aw, shit... you ain't really gonna use that thing, is you?'

'You wanna test me?' said Daisy, tightening her finger on the trigger of the gun that had no bullets.

'Hell no.'

'Then answer the question.' Daisy took a step towards her intruder, who immediately took a step further back, his hands in the air.

'I's... I's supposed to put the frighteners on you.'

'So your boss wants you to terrorise a helpless old lady?'

'Helpless?'

'That's beside the point. 'Frighten me into what?'

'Um...'

Daisy took another step closer, tightening the weapon against her shoulder, and giving him the meanest expression she could manage. 'Into what?'

'Um... into giving me the package. Geez, Finn said it would be a breeze.'

'Package? Finn?'

'Hell, lady. Or whatever you are. Can I have one question at a time, please?'

Daisy grinned menacingly. 'Ok... I don't have the package. I gave it to the police.'

'You did what?'

'You heard. Was it you who was supposed to pick it up?'

'Geez, no. I's just... just...'

'The errand boy?'

'Hell no. I's the muscle.'

Daisy looked him up and down. 'Seriously?'

'Ok, I's on probation. And you pointing that thing at me ain't helping my chances of promotion.'

'You poor thing. You want me to put in a good word with your boss?'

'Yeah... no... aw geez.'

'Well if you do want a reference, I need to know an address. So who's Finn?'

'Um... my boss...'

Daisy took a third step closer. Desmond took a third step back, making sure there was still ten feet between them. The woman brandishing the weapon shook her head. 'I think we've already established that, don't you? Finn who?'

'It's more than my life's worth, lady. I's already said too much.'

'More than your life's worth? So shall I shoot you now?'

Suddenly he looked like the cornered gazelle that was all out of options. Daisy saw the gloss of tears in his eyes reflecting in the lamplight, and the petrified rigidity of his body relax a little.

He was all out of options.

But then fate took a hand. Suddenly the outside security lights came on. For a moment, through the windows that still had their curtains open, the night was as bright as day. Her nerves already jangling, Daisy was distracted. In the second it took for her to glance through the front window, Desmond seized his moment.

She looked back, just in time to catch a flash of black-clad leg disappear through the outside kitchen doorway. She ran after him, but already knew there was nothing she could do. Even if there were any bullets in the gun she could hardly fire, not in Great Wiltingham late at night. And his ridiculously-long legs had already carried him away into the darkness of the street.

She lowered her arms, and let the rifle slide down to her thighs. And then, as she stood just outside the kitchen door feeling like she'd let a golden opportunity slip, she heard a noise. She jumped slightly as she felt something warm against her leg.

She bent down, and ruffled the fur on the back of Maisie's cat. 'Oh, Brutus... you do know how to make an entrance, don't you? You stole the limelight this time, for sure!'

The two of them wandered into the kitchen together. Daisy filled a small bowl with milk, and then placed it on the floor. Brutus looked grateful, and lapped it up.

Then she poured herself a very large brandy, and sat on her stool next to the island unit, lapping that up a little faster than she really should.

And then finally she let go of the tears of petrified relief; the ones she'd been determined not to cry for the last hour.

Chapter 18

Aidan rolled up at nine-thirty. Daisy was sitting on her stool at the island unit, her hands wrapped around a coffee cup, her eyes staring at nothing in particular. He knew straightaway something was wrong.

The AK-47 sitting on the countertop might have given him a clue.

'Daisy, what..?'

She slipped off the stool, wrapped her arms around him and buried her face in his shoulder. The words were small, almost a whisper. 'I think I might be getting too old for these kind of shenanigans, dear.'

'Shenanigans... tell me please?'

'I... someone was waiting for me when I got in last night.'

'You didn't... why didn't you call me?'

She tapped both hands on his shoulders, turned away. 'You know I've always tried to protect you from... that kind of thing. And no, I didn't shoot him. I didn't have time to load it... but, well, I have now. In case he came back.'

He stood behind her, wrapped arms around her waist and felt her lean back gratefully into him. 'Darling, you have to stop thinking like that. Those days are gone... well, they should be. You can't handle this alone. Although in truth, you shouldn't be handling it at all.'

She turned to him, kissed him on the cheek. 'I don't think I have a choice, Dip. It's got too close to home... rather literally, after last night.'

'So what... ok, I'll make you some Welsh... cheese on toast, while you tell me all about it.'

She told him all about it while he made her the comfort food they both knew was needed more than ever. He seemed to be shaking his head rather more than usual as he took in every word, and then put the automatic rifle back in its cupboard, and replaced it with the breakfast plate.

'So did you get any sleep at all?'

'Didn't even go to bed. He did run scared, but that didn't mean he wouldn't have come back.'

'Oh Daisy... you really should have called me. The least we could have done was to sit up the whole night together.'

She put down her fork, and as she looked up to him he saw the shine of mistiness in her eyes. 'I... I picked up the phone, but then something stopped me. I couldn't drag you into it.'

'So, you think you haven't dragged me into it already?'

'Oh... dear, I'm so sorry...'

She covered her eyes with her hands, and he pulled her close again. 'I didn't mean... we're in this heap of crap side by side, crazy woman. Whoever it is we're dealing with here, they must have seen us together, very likely on our way back from Matilda's that night. Obviously they now know where we both live, so we have to react to that.'

'Oh, I intend to, believe me.'

'No, Daisy. It's time to confess all to the police, so they can protect us.'

Her eyes narrowed as a stab of memory seared into her heart. 'Sure, like they did before, you mean?'

Aidan's stomach did a somersault inside him. Daisy might have put on a few years since her previous life, but that particular look had never changed. 'It... it's different now. We're different now.'

'Older but not wiser, maybe. And you know just as well as I do the police can't protect us, no matter how good their intentions are. There's no choice now but to protect ourselves.'

He groaned inside, but tried not to let Daisy see it on his face. He did know she was all too right. And he did know what Daisy meant by protecting themselves. 'I suppose you're going to tell me there's only one way to do that?'

She smiled, her fighting spirit beginning to return, helped by Aidan's presence and the cheese on toast with added ingredients. 'Unfortunately dear, there is only one way. We have to sort the bad guys out ourselves. Extinguish the threat, as it were.'

'I had a horrible feeling you were going to say that.'

'You don't have to be a part of it. Just go back to your little bungalow and do the Times crossword.'

'Very funny. From now on, I'm not letting you out of my sight, day or night.'

'I had a horrible feeling you were going to say that.'

He grinned, knowing she didn't mean a single word. 'So what now, before I go and fetch my pyjamas?'

'Well, Desmond might not be the brightest spark in the bonfire, but he did let slip who his boss was. Well, kind of.'

'Finn. That could be a first name, or a shortened one. Or a last name. Or a nickname.'

'Yes. But you don't get called Finn unless it's part of your name. It's not a lot to go on, but it is something, dear. So now we need Sarah and her database!'

– – –

Constable Sarah Lowry was at her desk when her mobile phone started to jump around in her pocket. She didn't recognise the number, but she recognised the voice on the other end.

'Daisy. Everything ok?'

The voice gave her a very brief rundown of recent events.

'Daisy!' she shrieked. Then she realised a couple of faces were glancing in her direction in a curious kind of way, and composed herself. 'Just a friend... nothing to worry about,' she called to them, forcing a somewhat unconvincing smile. Then she spoke into the phone in a more subdued voice.

'Daisy, do you want me to come?'

'No dear. I'm fine now. And don't tell anyone, especially Burrows, ok?'

'But... we should be involved... officially I mean. Protect you both.'

'Sarah, I mean it. Keep schtum, please. You know as well as I you can't protect us. But you can help.'

'Help? How?'

'The dozy punk let slip his boss was called Finn. Don't know if it's a first or last name. Maybe short for Finlay, Finbar, or something. Please will you feed it into the police database, see if anything comes up?'

She glanced around in a slightly guilty way, but the other officers present had lost interest. No one was looking at her like she was doing something she shouldn't. And it was Burrow's day off.

'Ok, but you know I'm not supposed to scan the database without good reason?'

'Sarah, this is good reason. Admittedly, not officially. Just run with it, ok?'

'And if I find something, then what?'

'Keep it to yourself, and then pop round later. Deal?'

'I suppose so. It is exciting... even if it's a more serious version of exciting now.'

'So just use that... excitement. Just don't get carried away with it and make someone else suspicious. This is under the radar, and right now needs to be kept that way.'

'I'm worried about you. What if they come back?'

'Desmond knows we don't have the package. And I scared the living daylights out of him, so I doubt they'll be back.'

'You scared him? How?'

'It doesn't matter. Maybe I threatened to run him over with my mobility scooter. Just get on that database, ok?'

Sarah shook her head. Whatever Daisy did, she wasn't giving. 'Ok. I'll pop round at teatime, and talk some sense into you.'

'Good luck with that.'

Sarah accessed the database, and searched for 'Finn'. A whole list of possible names came up, but as she brought up the details of each one, none of them seemed to fit the criteria. They were mostly petty criminals, none of whom were connected enough to be involved in drug smuggling.

Those who were connected to the underworld were already serving time. Two were deceased. Her heart sank as she reached the end of the list.

None of them were even vague candidates.

She closed her eyes, and tried to think logically. And then she had a thought. Maybe she had to widen the search, seek out people who weren't currently known to the police as criminals. She typed Finn, resident in Norfolk.

She knew it would bring up everyone who had even received a parking ticket. And sure enough it did. It wasn't as long a list as she'd envisaged, but as her eyes scrolled the names, her mouth went dry.

No, it couldn't be. He was a fine, upstanding citizen. And he lived not a million miles from where she did.

Just a few miles from where Daisy and Aidan did.

She shook her head, tried to tell herself she was clutching at very short straws. Daisy had told her not to get too excited. It had to be the new-found thrill of the chase, convincing her of things that could not possibly be.

But as the day wore on, and she tried to bring her heart-rate down with mundane police-type very boring things, she finally had to admit the heart was refusing to be brought down to a safe and unexcited level.

The man whose name kept reverberating around her skull had more than ample means to be involved in the one thing it seemed impossible he could be.

Chapter 19

Daisy smiled sweetly as the young woman who seemed far more familiar than she actually was walked through the kitchen door.

The smile was painted on, but the part of it that was happy to see her certainly wasn't. And the part of Sarah's smile, which tried to hide her simmering excitement, wasn't really hiding much at all.

'You found something then,' said Daisy as she narrowed her eyes into a question that wasn't a question at all.

'No... well, kind of...' She pulled Daisy into a tight hug, ripped the breath out of her. 'I can't believe you went through that...' Then her gaze switched to Aidan. 'And where were you?'

'Fast asleep,' he answered as he turned the steaks on the portable grill.

'What?'

Daisy eased herself away from Sarah, even though she really didn't want to. 'He didn't know. I didn't tell him until this morning.'

'Seriously?'

Aidan turned to them, waving the grilling prongs menacingly in the air. 'Indeed. And I'm just as pissed about it as you, Sarah.'

'You idiot.'

Daisy waved a dismissive hand in the air. 'Oh stop it, both of you. Can we just accept I'm a decrepit old geriatric and get on with it?'

'Decrepit? I doubt a certain Jamaican thug thinks that way.'

'Can we just get on with it?' Daisy repeated.

'Well, it won't happen again,' Aidan said as he loaded the sirloin steaks onto three plates, piled onion rings onto them, and went to the oven to grab the jacket potatoes and the tomatoes. 'I've moved in now.'

'Temporarily,' pointed out Daisy.

'I knew it,' said Sarah.

'Garden peas?' said Aidan.

'Can we just get on with it?' said Daisy for the third time, wanting to get on with it before anyone asked any more awkward questions.

'There are no criminals in the database with Finn in their name who could possibly fit into Mister Big's shoes.'

'Did you double-check?'

'Daisy!'

'Ok, so it's another dead end,' said Daisy dejectedly.

'Well, there was someone not a million miles from here with Finn in his name, but it's very unlikely to be him.'

'Why not?'

'Because he's an upstanding member of the local community. I only came across him because he got a speeding ticket a year ago.'

'So?'

'So he's a leading figure in country life around here. He gives to charity, supports conservation... and he lives just outside my village.'

'Do you know him?'

'Oh no... we move in completely different circles. He lives in a huge old house called Harrington Manor. It's in hundreds of acres.'

'So he enjoys his ill-gotten gains to the full.'

'Daisy... it was you who warned me about not getting too excited. It couldn't possibly be him.'

'What's his name?'

'Finlay Finnegan. Lord Finlay Finnegan.'

'Finlay Finnegan...' Daisy's eyes glazed over as she repeated the name in a whisper. 'Yes, it fits.'

'Fits what?'

'Well, he's got two reasons to shorten his name to Finn.'

'That'll never stand up in court,' Aidan grinned.

Daisy threw her eyes to the beamed ceiling. 'I know that, Dip. But...'

'Oh dear... that's another look I know,' Aidan groaned.

'Look?' said Sarah.

'Oh yes, the putting two and two together and making four and a half look.'

Sarah giggled, but Daisy didn't seem amused. 'Then you should know by now to listen to it, dear,' she said firmly.

'Oh, trust me I do.'

'Would someone like to let me in on your telepathic link please?'

Daisy put a hand on Sarah's arm. 'Sorry dear, it's just that I seem to have a sixth sense...'

'Seventh,' corrected Aidan.

'Whatever. An extra sense about some things. And you've just kicked it in.'

'I hope it's not painful.'

'Not yet, dear. But it might be.'

They finished the meal in virtual silence. Sarah wasn't sure if her new friends were lost in their telepathic link, but somehow it didn't seem it was her place to disturb them. Aidan didn't appear too distracted, but every now and then he would glance to Daisy. He said nothing, experience clearly telling him not to break the chain of whatever it was going on right then.

Daisy looked like she was somewhere else. Aidan seemed to know exactly where she was, but the other person at the table wasn't the slightest bit clairvoyant, and didn't have a clue where her friend had gone.

Then, finally, the silence was broken.

'Yes.'

'Yes?'

'Yes. It's him. Mister Big.'

Sarah looked at her wide-eyed. 'How can you possibly know that?'

'Dunno. I just do.'

'That'll never stand up in court either,' Aidan grinned as he stood up and stacked the plates.

'Do stop saying that, dear. Of course it won't. Which is why we have to make something happen that will.'

Halfway to the dishwasher, he stopped and looked back. 'Oh hell. I see a convoluted and somewhat dangerous plan looming.'

'Will somebody please...'

'Sarah, have forensics finished working at Jesse's caravan?'

'Yes, they've gone now. But we've taped it off; it's still a crime scene.'

'That's ok. I know what needs to be done, but first we need to go back and find Jesse's stash.'

'Daisy... they dug up the whole garden. There's no more flour there.'

Daisy looked at her like she was one of her students. 'Dear, whatever Jesse was, he wasn't stupid. He distanced himself as much as he could from his illicit activities, remember? So whatever stash he had in stock, it wouldn't be kept at the caravan.'

'So it could be anywhere then?'

105

Daisy shook her head. 'Not anywhere. He'd keep it near to hand, somewhere he could access it without anyone knowing.'

Aidan turned away from the dishwasher, and leant on the island countertop on his forearms. 'But that trailer park is an ants' nest of humanity. It wouldn't be there, surely?'

'His caravan is right up against the perimeter hedge, isn't it?'

'Ah'

'Ah? Am I missing something here, yet again?' cried Sarah.

Aidan put her out of her misery. 'The field next door to the park. Daisy thinks it's somewhere there.'

'I guarantee there's a hidden hole in that hedge.'

'How... yes there is. I went through it myself, looked around. It's just a farmer's field.'

'But you didn't know then what you know now,' Daisy grinned.

'I don't know much more now, but I guess you're going to enlighten me?' Sarah pouted.

'Let's just say, Aidan and me need to go gardening again. Tomorrow night, early hours of the morning, sound about right?'

Chapter 20

Daisy spent most of the next day in the office. It was nothing to do with her automatic rifle, which stayed firmly in its cabinet. There was something much more important she had to do, on the PC.

She sent Aidan to work on the garden, cutting the lawn and doing a little weeding. As she said to him, there was no village gardener to do it now, and if someone didn't keep on top of it, the beautiful outside space would go to wrack and ruin.

He wasn't easily fooled, knew she wanted him out of the way while she did something he wasn't yet privileged to see. But he also knew there was little choice, and that once she'd done what she needed to, she would tell him all about it.

So he made himself scarce, even though the slightly dull ache in his stomach told him she was cooking something up that might not be too good for their health.

Daisy was cooking something up, and she was just as aware as Aidan the plan brewing in her mind had the potential to boil over, and end up causing a hell of a mess.

It wouldn't have to matter. Now that things had got personal, for Daisy there was no choice other than to pile all the ingredients into the frying pan, and hope none of them spat back out into the fire.

They shared lunch together on the patio terrace. It was a beautiful late-August day; not as hot as it had been, but easily warm enough to enjoy the open air, even though it was starting to cloud over as they finished eating.

Aidan glanced into the darkening sky, said he'd better finish his work before it rained, and ambled off to weed a few more flower beds. Daisy went back inside, and carried on tapping keys.

It was just gone three when the office door eased open, and he walked in. Engrossed in her work, her eyes planted firmly on the PC monitor, Daisy didn't even realise he was there until he spoke.

'Starting to spit, dear. But I've done what you wanted me out of the way for.' He narrowed his eyes at the screen. 'What on Earth..?'

She looked round, a little startled he was there. 'It's my new identity, darling,' she confessed.

He studied the website on the screen. 'Seriously? Redrum House?'

'It's rather good, don't you think?'

'Um... apart from the fact it's been done before... what?'

'I've created a simple website on Wordpress. Looks convincing, doesn't it?'

'I'm not going to like this, am I?'

'Probably not.'

'And where did that old house come from? It's sure not this cottage.'

'Of course it isn't. It's just a random picture I found on the internet.'

'Daisy! You can't just pass off someone else's home as your own!'

'Don't worry. This website will only need to be live for a few days.'

'That's not really what I...'

'Look, dear. I've put a picture of me on there too.' She scrolled down a little.

Aidan gasped. 'But... Lady Rose Busch? You can't be serious...'

'Oh I am, dear. It's all part of the subterfuge. I believe people used to call it a sting.'

He gaped at her open-mouthed. 'I... but... this time you've gone too far, Daisy. I know that once upon a time you used to...'

'I've SEO'd it as well, dear. So when he googles it, it will show up clear as day.'

'Um... he?'

'Finlay Finnegan. He'll check me out, of course.'

'He will? Oh Daisy... no...'

She stood up, slipped her arms around his waist and smiled a reassuring smile, which failed dismally to hit its mark. 'Darling, he's the Mister Big around here. And he didn't get to be where he is by being careless. The police don't stand a hope in hell of banging him up for anything more than a speeding offence. The only way to bring him down is to do it on his own terms.'

He held her tight, because he could do no other. 'You're not explaining things very well, but my gut seems to know one thing is as clear as glass.'

'I did say you wouldn't like it.'

'Darling, you may see this as too close to home in more than one way, but shouldn't we let someone else handle it?'

His voice was small, tempered by the fact he already knew the answer to that particular question. Daisy caressed his cheek, kissed him gently. 'I don't need to reply to that, do I?'

He let out a resigned sigh. 'No, dear. Just tell me what your insane plan is.'

She sat back down on the office chair. 'Finnegan obviously distances himself from the entire operation, so he can be seen as a fine upstanding citizen. I suspect his role is literally bulk supply. He accesses the goods, but then gets others to do everything else, relinquishing a little of his profit to them, in order to stay squeaky-clean. He now believes he's been double-crossed by Jesse, his wholesale distributer. Whoever Jesse supplied got seriously pissed off, and Jesse's demise has left a hole in Finnegan's network. So he needs to do something about it, before he gets left with goods he doesn't want hanging around, and possibly incriminating him.'

'That all makes sense. But how does that help us?'

'I'm going to offer to be his new distributer!'

'You? Oh no... Lady Rose Busch?'

'Dear, do you have any idea what percentage of the English aristocracy are actually criminals?'

'That's not the point.'

'Of course it is. Lady Rose lives in Redrum house, close to Great Yarmouth. She's a junkie aristocrat who's snorted away her money, and now needs funds to bolster up her finances.'

'He'll never believe it.'

'He will if I have the right ammunition.'

'Daisy, guns aren't the answer.'

'Well dear, now and again they are, but this time I'm referring to something else.'

'You've lost me.'

'I need to go visit him, and show him I'm already experienced in that particular commodity. Which is why tonight, we have to find Jesse's stash.'

'Oh dear.'

Daisy wrinkled up her nose. 'Now go and have a shower, dear. You smell of dandelions.'

Daisy spent a little while making sure she had as much internet presence as possible. Then she swallowed hard, gritted her teeth, and picked up the phone. Finlay Finnegan's public persona had a telephone number there for all to see.

Just as she heard the dialling tone, Aidan appeared in the office doorway. As someone answered, she reached for the comfort of his hand.

'Harrington Manor. Can I help you?'

Daisy swallowed hard again, and put on her posh voice. 'Yes. May I speak with Lord Finnegan, please?'

'May I ask who is calling, please?'

'Lady Rose Busch.'

'Um... I'm sorry? I didn't quite catch that.'

She saw Aidan pull a silly face out of the corner of her eye, ignored it. 'Yes you did. Who is this?'

'I'm Johnson, Lord Finnegan's butler and personal assistant. He doesn't take unsolicited calls I'm afraid, Lady... um, Busch.'

She noticed Aidan shaking his head, but ignored that too. 'Well, he'll want to take this one. Put me through to him please, you insolent man.'

He didn't exactly sound fazed by the insult. 'I'm sorry, no can do. And he's out of the country right now anyway.'

'Oh. When is he back?'

The voice on the end hesitated a moment. 'Sometime tomorrow, your Ladyship. He's likes to be back for his regular Thursday clay pigeon shoot at midday.'

'Oh, I say. I do enjoy a pigeon shoot. I assume it takes place in the grounds?'

'Indeed. But it is a private event. Invitation only, I'm afraid.'

111

'You do seem to be afraid of rather a lot of things, Johnson. So tell him I'm inviting myself. I am rather a good shot after all... and I need to discuss some important business with him.'

She put the phone down before the unfortunate man could be afraid of anything else, and then turned to Aidan.

'It seems Mister Finnegan is out of the country until tomorrow. I wonder what he's doing?'

'Maybe he's on holiday?'

'Sure he is. And that butler sounded like Vinnie Jones putting on a posh accent.'

'Vinnie Jones doesn't do posh accents.'

'Exactly... curiouser and curiouser...'

'That'll never stand up in...'

'Oh do shut up, dear. Just let me wallow in my suspicious nature.'

'That sounds dangerous. So what has your suspicious nature deduced?'

'That it's game on, dear.'

Chapter 21

It was just after eleven when Daisy emerged from the bedroom. They'd both decided a couple of hours sleep was a good idea, but given the anticipation of the task ahead, neither had managed anything that could be described as proper sleep.

It had rained quite heavily for three hours, but as the early evening turned to night the clouds had blown away, and a bright three-quarter moon pooled its light over their little part of Norfolk.

Aidan, pouring water into two mugs to make resuscitating coffees, grinned when he saw her walk in. She was dressed in the prerequisite midnight gardening outfit, but this time with rather huge builder's boots on her feet.

'You look like a covert Minnie Mouse.'

'And you look like a cat burglar, but I was too polite to say anything.'

He grinned. 'I guess we're both burglars... if there's anything to burgle.'

'Only one way to find out. Is that coffee?'

He handed her the mug. Ten seconds later the outside security lights came on. They glanced to each other in an uneasy kind of way, and fell silent, listening. But then the sound of gravel crunching on driveway filled their ears, and headlights flashed across the window.

'Well, if Desmond's back, he's not doing a very good job of taking us by surprise.'

They both knew it wasn't their favourite thug, but who it was arriving just before midnight was making them curious. They headed together out of the side door. A familiar car had stopped in front of the garage, its boot lid up. Then it slammed shut, and the slim figure came into view and leant on her shovel, like all the best gardeners do.

'I figured the King and Queen of Spades could do with a hand,' she grinned.

'More like a couple of jokers,' Aidan said ruefully.

'Sarah!' said Daisy, a slight smile on her face. 'You really shouldn't be here.'

'And you shouldn't be doing what you're doing at your age, you interfering old codgers.'

'It's ok, my mobility scooter will make it up to the field,' Daisy retorted, feeling a mixture of regret and joy that she'd told Sarah of their plans.

'So how long have we got?' she grinned back.

'Over an hour yet. We've just made coffee. You up for one?'

'You bet. Oh wow, this is so exciting!'

The hands on the clock flicked to one o'clock. The three of them piled into the BMW, and Aidan drove along the silent and deserted village main street, heading for the trailer park.

Sarah had made it very clear she was going nowhere except where they were, so Daisy hadn't even pointed out that if they got caught, it wouldn't look so good on her police CV.

Then she told herself it was nothing to do with the fact she was quite glad to have Sarah there, even though deep down she knew it probably was.

Aidan drove slowly past the trailer park, and then pulled into the small opening between the road and the gate to the field. 'Well, here we are,' he said, like it was necessary to tell the others.

114

Daisy and Sarah were already climbing out of the car, and three seconds later the boot lid was open, and spades and torches were grabbed.

'Come on,' said Daisy in another stage whisper, heading over to the gate, and then stopping in her tracks. 'Sod it.'

'What?' said Sarah.

'It's padlocked. Oh well, easy enough to climb over.'

She placed a builder's boot on the first bar, lifted herself up. Aidan flashed his torch over the gate. 'Dear, be careful. It's a bit mossy, and it's been raining.'

'Dip, please stop clucking like a mother hen. I'm not stu...'

The words disappeared. So did Daisy. A millisecond later there was a splashy kind of thud. Followed by a verbal description of her feelings.

'Bugger.'

'That's my line,' grinned Aidan, leaning over the gate to give a slightly-soggy Daisy a hand to her feet. 'I told you it had been raining.'

'How was I supposed to know mossy gates are lethal in the wet?'

'I tried to...'

'Now look at me. I'm saturated.'

'At least your woolly hat is still on.'

'Is that supposed to make me feel better? Or drier?' she hissed.

Sarah pointed out they really should get on with it, so Daisy shook her head in a sheepish kind of way, and the other two midnight cowboys joined her in the field. They, however, negotiated the offending gate a little more carefully.

'Right... this way,' said Daisy, as she squelched over to the hedge separating the field from the trailer park.

115

Aidan groaned. 'There's a lot of hedge to dig under.'

'Please whisper, dear. There are people sleeping just the other side of it.'

He nodded. 'There's a lot...'

'Yes, dear, we heard you the first time. But I think we can disregard most of the hedge.'

'What... what do you mean?'

'As I said before, Jesse will make sure he keeps his stash close to home.'

They made their way along the hedgerow. It was a typical Norfolk-type farm hedgerow, the hedge itself raised up slightly on a low bank, made to look higher than it was by a drainage ditch right in front of it.

The ditch had been bone dry for four weeks. Until that day. Three hours of heavy rain falling on sun-baked ground had struggled to soak in. But it had to go somewhere. As she flashed her torch along the drainage ditch, the beam reflecting off the standing water, Sarah groaned.

'I really should have stayed in bed.'

'Glad you didn't,' Daisy whispered. 'But look, there's Jesse's hole.'

As they slunk over to it, they could see that a much darker patch in the line of hedge was indeed a hole. And it was right on the corner of the trailer park. In the moonlight, they could see the roof of Jesse's caravan just the other side.

'Do we start digging now?'

'No, wait. Let me think.' Daisy moved closer to the ditch, panned her torch along the low bank just the other side of it. Sarah was nodding her head, her police training putting her on the same wavelength. She answered Aidan's curious glance with a whispered reply.

'Jesse wasn't going to make it too difficult to access his stash. If you know what to look for, it might be obvious.'

'If there's a stash at all.'

'True.'

'Ah.'

Daisy's whispered exclamation got them running over to her.

'I think I've found it.'

Two more torches joined Daisy's. With the extra light, all three of them could see quite easily that a rectangular piece of rough grass on the low bank, right next to the hedge, had come away very slightly.

The rain might have been responsible for Daisy's rather embarrassing tumble, and the fact she ended up rather muddy. But it had also helped to wash away a little of the soil around the neatly-cut rectangle of coarse turf, and make it slightly more obvious to anyone who was actually looking for it.

Aidan's face broke into his lop-sided grin. 'It's got to be under that.'

'So what are you waiting for?'

Sarah was already splashing through the ditchwater, and grabbing the rectangle with her gloved hands. 'Wow, it's heavy.'

Aidan joined her. 'The rain hasn't helped.' Together they moved the slab of rough grass to the side.

'Oh.'

'What?' hissed Daisy from the other side of the ditch, reluctant to get any wetter.

'It's just soil.'

'Well, he's not going to make it too obvious, is he?' She handed Aidan a spade, and as he stabbed it into the soil, it hit something hard.

They all looked at each other, but the freeze-frame only lasted a second. Daisy passed Sarah her spade, and together they dug around the oblong box like their life depended on it.

'It's an old metal military dispatch box,' said Aidan.

Finally they could lift out the dark green box by its handle, and then splash back through the ditchwater to reach Daisy. The three of them crouched around it, like it was red hot.

'Well, go on then... lift the lid.'

Slowly, Aidan did as he was asked. The dispatch box was the perfect size to fit four bags of flour. There weren't four bags in it. But there were two.

'Result,' grinned Daisy.

'Um... guys...' said Sarah.

'Yes, I know. We should hand it over to the authorities.'

'Well, yes you should. But that wasn't what I was going to say.'

'Sarah?'

'Um... don't look now, but there's a great big four-legged thing with horns taking an unnerving kind of interest in us.'

Very slowly, Aidan turned his head. The bull was about fifty yards away, and watching the rather unexpected sight with a menacing kind of intense stare. Quietly he closed the lid on the box. 'Just move, very slowly, towards the gate. Don't make any sudden movements, and it will be fine.'

It wasn't fine. It probably would have been, except that as they began to move slowly towards the gate, the friendly bull decided to amble towards them, a little bit faster than they were moving.

And with the best will in the world, when a pair of sharp horns was on cruise mode in their direction, and safety was just twenty yards away, moving slowly has a tendency to go out of the window.

And so does keeping dry. As the running figures reached the gate, the deep puddle between them and safety didn't seem to matter so much. The three even-soggier midnight gardeners slithered over the gate, and piled back into the car.

And as the old bull, who really just wanted to say hello, stopped ambling and watched curiously, still no nearer to understanding why three odd-looking humans were in his field in the early hours of the morning, the car sped away.

'Did anyone bring the stash?' gasped Daisy.

'Course I did,' said Aidan. 'And you'd better help clean up the inside of this car in the morning.'

Chapter 22

Maisie's cat Brutus followed the three humans into the kitchen, thinking all his Christmases had come at once. It was most unusual to find humans up in the early hours of the morning, and give him milk twice in one week. Then he saw the state of them, and beat a hasty retreat, thinking that it wasn't merry at all, just A Christmas Horror Story.

Daisy sank onto her stool, pulled off the very muddy boots. 'Well dears, I think that was a success, if a rather soggy one.'

Aidan nodded a resigned kind of agreement as he spread a newspaper on the island unit, and placed the soil-covered dispatch box onto it. Sarah wiped a spot of mud off her cheek. 'I should go, give you guys some peace.'

'Won't your parents wonder why you're arriving home at three in the morning?'

'It's ok. I told them I was staying the night at a friend's house in Kings Lynn.'

'Boyfriend?'

'Oh... no. No time for such things, when you're a career girl like me.'

Daisy threw a slight smile to Aidan. 'I thought that too, until I found out it's important to make time for those things. But won't this friend wonder why you're turning up looking like you've been mud-wrestling?'

'I'm not really staying with a friend... I'll grab a little sleep in the car, and then go straight to work.'

'Oh no you won't.' Daisy glanced to Aidan, who gave her an almost-imperceptive nod. 'The spare bed is made up. Go get yourself a shower, and then you can use the small bedroom.'

'Oh, I can't impose. I only came to make sure you two didn't get into trouble... fat lot of use that was.'

'Nobody could have predicted heavy rain and rampant bulls, my dear. But the last thing you're doing right now is sleeping in the car in that state. Aidan will show you where your room is. The shower is en suite. I'm getting a nice warm bath. You joining me, dear?'

Sarah allowed Aidan to show her the room. He told her there was a dressing gown in the wardrobe if she needed it, and then wished her a good night, quietly excused himself, and left to join Daisy.

She looked curiously at her surroundings. The room was one of two on the first floor. The window wall was just over half-height, the front third of the beamed ceiling angling down to meet it. Built partway into the roof of the eighteenth century cottage, it was a cosy room, the white walls and natural oak beams giving it a warmth that made her feel it was a comforting place to spend time in.

A double bed with a padded headboard sat against one wall, with a multi-coloured leaded glass lamp standing on a white-painted bedside table next to it, casting gentle rays of light around the small room, and giving the white walls faint shades of every colour in the rainbow.

On the side wall, a white-painted free-standing wardrobe was full of clothes, and as she ran a hand across the hangers, she could see they weren't Daisy's.

She closed the doors quickly, feeling strangely guilty that she'd looked inside. On the low window wall, a run of cupboards filled the floor space, a kneehole in the centre with a padded stool forming a dressing table. She slid open one of the drawers. There were clothes there too.

Each side of the dormer window, a small shelf was fixed at the joint of the half-height wall and the eaves ceiling. There was nothing on either shelf except two small framed pictures. Sarah frowned as she picked one of them up, and sat on the bed so the light would help her see it better.

Other than the clothes in the wardrobe and drawers, there were no personal items in the room. Yet the dull, very faint ache in her stomach made her feel like she was trespassing in someone else's space.

She looked at the photo frame in her hands. And suddenly realised she was indeed in someone else's room.

The picture had been taken some time ago. The three people in it looked happy, their wide smiles posed for the camera, but clearly not at all fake.

She recognised two of them instantly. A few years younger, Daisy and Aidan were standing either side of the third person in the picture, their arms around her, in the way parents do. The girl between them, in her mid-teens, looked familiar too, although Sarah didn't know her at all.

The girl looked very much like she did at that age.

She dropped the photo to her lap, and wiped away a tear that had just appeared for seemingly no reason. She sniffed back more tears as she cast her eyes around the room. She was in someone else's space. Someone who wasn't in it anymore. Or might never have been.

She'd noticed Aidan's faint nod when Daisy had glanced at him, telling her it was okay to offer their guest the room. At the time she'd thought nothing of it, but now she realised its significance. They'd invited her to use it, even though in doing so they knew she would see things hardly anyone else ever had.

Something awful had clearly gone down, a few years ago. But the room wasn't a shrine. It was like it was just there, kept clean and pristine, ready and waiting for the day that special someone would come to occupy it once more.

Sarah dragged herself to the feet that had suddenly become heavy. If she didn't grab a much-needed shower right then, she'd fall asleep before she grabbed it at all. Daisy and Aidan clearly knew there would be questions, but they would have to wait for another time.

She opened the planked pine door to the en suite, and turned on the shower.

Fifteen minutes of cascading power-shower water revived her a little, as well as washing away the dirt of a soggy Norfolk field. She dried herself off, slipped on the gown, and then glanced at herself in the mirror. She looked more like herself.

And even more like the girl in the photograph.

She was thirsty. There didn't seem to be a glass anywhere in the room, so she decided to head downstairs and grab one from the kitchen. Pausing a moment on the small landing, she listened for any sounds from Daisy's room. All was silent; it seemed like she and Aidan were sleeping peacefully.

As she crept quietly down the stairs, she discovered she was wrong. There were lights on, and as she reached the kitchen area, both of them were there.

'Guys, I'm sorry...'

'Oh.' Daisy looked round, and as she saw Sarah in the gown, her face was a combination of joy and pain. She swallowed hard, obvious enough to anyone who knew the reason why. 'It's ok, Sarah dear. We were just musing over the spoils while we grabbed a coffee before we went to bed.'

'I was thirsty, just came to get some water. Oh, I say...'

The lid on the dispatch box was open. The two bags of flour were next to it, sitting quietly and innocently on the island countertop.

'Yes, indeed,' said Aidan as he handed her a glass. 'It's difficult to work out how many ruined lives are contained in those two parcels, but it has to be an awful lot.'

Sarah looked wide-eye at the packages. 'What...'

'Yes I know, dear. You must hand them over to your boss. But please, not for a couple of days.'

'A couple of days?'

Aidan was shaking his head as he spoke. 'Daisy has a plan. Although if you ask me...'

'Dear, you have a brain the size of a small planet, but just now and then you have to let us meteorites have our moment in the sun.'

'You know what happens to meteorites that fly too close to the sun.'

'Daisy? What are you cooking up now?'

'Come and sit down,' Daisy said, offering the stool next to her. 'The day after tomorrow... well, tomorrow now, given the late hour... our fine upstanding lord is having a clay pigeon shoot at the manor. And I'm going to be there...'

Chapter 23

'Oh my god... you look like something out of an Agatha Christie novel... or a character from a Cluedo board.'

'Don't you recognise the outfit?' Daisy grinned.

'It rings a vague bell from somewhere in the distance past.'

'These are the clothes I wore when I had to get close to another bent aristocrat, rather a long time ago.'

'I'm surprised they still fit.'

'Now you're being insolent, Dip. Of course they fit... if I don't do up the jacket buttons.'

'Hmm...' He looked over the vision in tweed. An old-style white blouse with a rounded collar was topped by a dark-green tweed waistcoat, texture-patterned with some kind of flowers. A matching tweed jacket wrapped around her shoulders, and an almost-matching deerstalker hat struggled to contain Daisy's silver curls. A pair of beige breeches almost completed the look, but the final touch forced him to let out an amused laugh.

'Pink flower-patterned wellies, dear? And breeches?'

She gave him a disgruntled glare. 'It's been raining again. And they're not breeches, just a pair of plain sweatpants tucked into the wellies. Lady Rose is a dotty aristocrat, remember? But she's quite sane really, even if she is a junkie. She's got connections in the right trade, but she's also somewhat rich and eccentric, like most aristocrats. I based her on a posh version of Maisie.'

'Knowing Maisie, she'd be quite pleased if she knew.'

'Hopefully she never will. But it shouldn't be too difficult to get into character, if I think of Maisie's approach to life.

Lady Rose isn't the type to take no for an answer, dippy as she is.'

'So you're right then, it won't be too difficult to get into character.'

'I'll ignore that remark, Henderson.'

'Yes, ma'am. Sorry ma'am.' He tipped his hat, and then shook his head in a slightly despairing way.

Daisy matched his shake. 'Really though, Henderson. Is a baseball cap the right attire for a shoot?'

'Would you rather I wore a top hat and penguin suit?'

'Ok, point taken. You are only my butler after all.'

'Playing your butler, m'lady.'

'Of course. Now let's get going, or we'll be late.' The pink wellies trotted off in the direction of the car. 'You did pack my gun I assume, Henderson?'

'Wow, look at this place.'

As soon as they drove through the oversized brick pillars of the entrance to Harrington Manor, the impressive facade of the big old house dominated the view. It looked to be over a hundred feet wide, and three storey's high. Yet another floor was built halfway into the pantiled roof, its gabled windows arranged one next to the other, like sentinels.

Georgian-paned windows looked like the job of repainting them would be equal to repainting the Forth Bridge. In the centre of the ivy-covered grey brick frontage, a pillastered arch sheltered a tall pair of very solid wood doors with heavy brass fittings.

'Look at those cars,' said Daisy, trying not to sound too overwhelmed.

On the large, rolled-gravel forecourt, it looked like an advert for luxury car hire. Three Range Rovers with private plates were accompanied by an Aston Martin, a vintage Rolls Royce, and a Lamborghini.

'No prizes for guessing which one is Finns,' said Aidan as he shook his head yet again.

'Let's just get this over with,' said Daisy grimly.

Aidan stopped the car right next to the Rolls, and they climbed out. Low buildings flanked each side of the forecourt. One flank looked like residential accommodation, likely for the live-in staff. The other flank had a run of large white-painted doors, and appeared to be an old stable block.

Daisy paused for a moment, listening for any sounds of horses, but there were none. It seemed her mark preferred horsepower of a different kind.

A big, brick-built archway was built into the ornate wall next to the left corner of the house, and through it they could see formal gardens. 'Let's go that way. Best not to waste time introducing ourselves to the staff.'

Aidan grabbed the gun bag from the boot, and they strolled through to the immaculately-kept formal gardens. 'Capability Brown must have had a hand or two in this,' mused Daisy as they slipped down the far side of the rectangular beds and coiffured lawns separated by very low yew hedging. They headed for a second arch in a tall wall two hundred yards away, which looked like it led to the less-formal sloping meadows.

As they emerged onto the top meadow, a beautiful country vista filled their eyes. That part of Norfolk wasn't as flat as some of the county, and rolling low green hills in the distance were dotted with copses and larger areas of woodland. A little nearer, a small natural lake reflected the rays of the late-summer sun, a tiny white-painted boathouse only just big enough for rowing boats and sailing dinghies sitting on its near bank.

Beyond that, the horizon was filled with the darker green of a much larger wood, stretching as far as their eyes could see. The whole scene was beautiful and impressive, a combination of natural wonder and managed parkland that delighted their eyes.

But they weren't there to be delighted. And nearer to them, standing on the gently-sloping parkland four hundred yards away, was a stark reminder of that. Their fine upstanding host, accompanied by five of his equally-rich pals, lifted his shooting rifle into the air and cried, 'Pull!'

The twang of the catapult filled the air, and a disc of clay fired into the sky. The crack of a rifle reverberated between the copse and the house, followed by a cry of disappointment.

'Damn it! Missed!'

Someone called out. 'Never mind, old boy. Can't hit every one.'

His lordship looked like he believed he should hit every one, and handed the gun to his man to reload. And then he looked round curiously, as a cry of a different kind filled the air.

'Cooeee... cooeee!'

A strange-looking woman in pink wellies was ambling towards him, grinning like a Cheshire cat, and waving like she was demented. He looked at Johnson, who shrugged his shoulders and said, 'This might just be the peculiar woman who phoned the other day, Finn.'

The grinning woman reached him, and gasped out the words breathlessly. 'Lord Finnegan, I presume? Soo pleased to meet you.'

'I'm sorry, did I invite you? Who the hell are you anyway?'

Daisy looked him over, without him knowing she was. The shooting attire was pristine, and fitted perfectly. His black hair just covered the top of his ears, and seemed to flow in faintly-wavy locks. The face that some women would find handsome was shrouded by carefully-trimmed three-day stubble. His vaguely-amused smile looked genuine, but somehow conveyed a hidden menace that wasn't going to be argued with.

His voice was clipped, trained to speak in the proper way that would impress those in the circles he moved in, officially at least. But a faint southern-Irish tint had failed to quite leave his accent. Daisy knew straightaway she'd have to bustle her way into his life, and not give him time to think too much. Anything less and she'd be carted away without a second thought.

'I'm soo sorry. No, I invited myself. I did tell your miserable butler I was coming. Oh sorry, I'm Rose. Lady Rose Busch.'

'Seriously?'

'You'd better believe it.'

'I'm sorry, Lady... Busch, but this is a private shoot. I'm afraid you'll have to leave.'

'Oh don't be silly, dear. Look, I've brought my own gun!' She turned to her clearly long-suffering butler, and grabbed the gun bag. 'Shall we get on with it?'

Chapter 24

His lordship looked a little bemused by the onslaught of rather loud words. So did the other members of the shooting party, all of whom seemed a little too amused by the unexpected turn of events to bother coming to their host's rescue.

He threw a defeated hand into the air. 'Alright. It will be time to lunch soon, anyway. Just... just do what the rest of us do, ok?'

'Of course. I am a good shot, you know.' Daisy bent over and began to unzip the gun bag. As she did, a flash of something coming from the copse two hundred yards away caught her eye. She glanced up to Aidan. 'Someone's watching us,' she whispered. 'I just saw the flash of sunlight reflecting off his binoculars.'

No one else seemed to have noticed it. Someone shouted, 'pull', and as the clayman did his job the disc flew into the air. The crack of a rifle was followed by it shattering into a multitude of pieces.

'Good shot, Charles,' someone said.

Five more times a disc soared into the air, and two more times it shattered into fragments. Daisy kept half an eye on the undergrowth of the copse, but there were no further signs of someone watching them. Then her attention was diverted, as her aristocratic host addressed her.

'So, Lady Rose, would you be liking a try?'

He had a faintly-amused smirk on his face, which was tantamount to a red rag where Daisy was concerned. 'Thought you'd never ask.'

She shrieked out the command to the clayman. Just as the disc flew into the air, she pulled her weapon from the bag, stood up quickly, and fired a volley of ten shots from the AK-47. The first bullet shattered the disc. The other nine likely would have as well, except there was nothing left to shatter.

It had the desired effect. As the thunderous noise reverberated around the meadow and died away to silence, all eyes were upon her.

'Got it!' she said, like it was the most natural thing in the world.

The silence was as deafening as the noise had been a few moments ago. But finally, someone found a small voice.

'I say, old girl. Isn't that tantamount to cheating?'

Lord Finnegan closed his mouth, but then opened it again to stutter out a few words. 'Where... where the hell did you get that thing from?'

'I have connections. So now do I have your attention?'

'Um... I...' He turned to the others. 'Gentlemen, I... I think it is time to take lunch. Please make your way to the house.'

Daisy slipped the weapon back into its bag, and then shoved it into her butler's arms. 'Take this to the car, Henderson. And then go find the staff kitchen. Someone there will no doubt feed you. I may be some time.'

For a second he looked at her like he could throttle her, but then realised stage one of the plan had been a success, so said, 'Yes Ma'am,' and turned away meekly. But just as she watched him go, apologising silently for having to talk to him that way, another flash of sunlight on binoculars caught her eye. Luckily every one of her companions and their men were heading away from the copse, so no one else saw it.

131

Lord Finnegan was looking at her with a little more respect. 'Perhaps, my fair lady, we should make our way to the office, so we can talk in private?'

'Thought you'd never ask!'

The good lord led the way to his office, which turned out to be more like a library. The large room had two big windows overlooking the formal gardens, framed on the outside by yellow wisteria bushes that looked like exterior curtains. On the rear wall were large bookcases, built from floor to the very high ceiling, and crammed with first editions Daisy doubted he'd ever read. Most of the varnished wooden floor was covered with a fine-quality rug, which Daisy made sure she walked over in her wellington boots, as heavily as she could.

He looked with some dismay at the trail of muddy prints. Daisy tried to look as distraught as she could pretend. 'Oh, I'm soo sorry. I'm such a pillock sometimes.'

He tried to wave it off. 'No matter. I am sure Isobella has some kind of cleaner that will get soil off a Persian rug.'

'Oh, I say. Now I feel really bad.'

He shook his head, and indicated a damask-covered chair standing on the opposite side of the big mahogany desk he then sat himself behind. The desk didn't seem to have anything on it other than a keyboard and computer monitor.

The door knocked, he called to whoever it was to enter, and a pretty, obviously-foreign maid in a smart black and white uniform walked in with a large silver tray, and placed it on the desk. On the way out she looked with some horror at the trail of muddy footprints on the Persian rug.

Finn lifted two of the silver dome-shaped lids, and dug a solid-silver teaspoon into a small bowl he'd revealed.

'Would you be liking some caviar and crackers, Rose?' he asked.

'Good god, no. Disgusting stuff. Do people really still eat that vulgar crap? One step off foie gras if you ask me. And do you really want to suffer with secondary amyloidosis?'

'The connection hasn't been proven, Rose. And... well, we've all got to die sometime.'

'Ah well, that's a very true statement, dear boy. But just for now, do you have any pork pie?'

He shook his head. 'I'm afraid not. It's full of saturated fat, you know.'

She laughed, in a slightly sarcastic way. 'Says he, consuming fish eggs and poisonous duck livers.'

'Whatever. So what can I be doing for you, Rose?'

'Actually, dear boy, it's more about what I can do for you.'

Daisy saw his eyes narrow, and noticed him lean forward slightly in his chair. She'd got his undivided attention, but balancing the fine line between successfully completing stage two and taking a step too far was going to be tricky.

He spoke slowly, deliberately. 'And what makes you think you can do something for me that would be worth my time?'

She smiled a confident smile, which was a million miles away from what she was really feeling. Aidan was somewhere the other side of the house, and her weapon was in the car... equally as far away. She'd never get to either of them if a quick escape was called for.

And then she caught a flash of something moving, just outside one of the windows. Then it disappeared, but five seconds later the top part of a familiar face was pressed up against the bottom pane, peering intently at them over the window cill.

Luckily the desk with Finn behind it was facing away from the windows. He hadn't seen anything. But if he decided to stand up and walk around, he surely would. There was nothing else for it but to put her cards on the table right then, and just hope her poker face would bring a satisfactory end result. She sucked in a deep breath, trying not to let him see she was, and then switched on a confident smile for the benefit of both the people who were watching her intently.

'Well let me see, dear boy. For starters... I know all about your secret little sideline.'

Chapter 25

Sarah watched through the window for a minute, and then felt a little easier about things. Daisy was sitting in the private office with Finn, smiling away as they talked. She didn't seem to be in any immediate danger.

Satisfied, she disentangled herself from the wisteria branches, and stepped quickly back to the path.

Right next to someone who didn't look very pleased to find her there.

'So just what are you doing?'

'I...um... making sure everything is ok.'

He narrowed his eyes. 'And is it?'

'Yes, I think so. Daisy looks... smiley.'

'That doesn't mean anything. Especially as you're the one endangering the whole operation.'

'I... I wasn't. It's my duty to protect you both.'

'Walk with me. Just look innocent. The guests might think you're a maid or something. I only came out for a smoke. Good job I did. What the hell, Sarah?'

She glanced down to the thin brown tube between his fingers. They walked together to the corner of the building. 'I'm sorry, Aidan. I had to do something. Just keep an eye on you, and be there if something went wrong.'

'Sarah, your intentions are honourable. But quite frankly it was very nearly you who was responsible for things going wrong.'

'I don't understand.'

'Daisy saw the sun glinting off your binoculars while you were hiding in the copse. Luckily for us all, no one else did.'

'Oh. I see.'

'And if you saw Daisy's smiling face through the office window, then she definitely saw you. Luckily again, Finn didn't. If he had, we'd be surrounded by thugs with lethal weapons right now.'

'Oh. I see.'

'Yes, I hope you do. Daisy is way better... equipped than you to handle this kind of thing.'

'Yeah, I saw the antics with the automatic rifle.'

They reached the gravel forecourt. Aidan put a gentle hand on her arm. 'That's just a relic from a bygone era, Sarah. But you might be advised not to tell Daisy that. Now go... slip away quietly before you blow the whole operation to bits. But... but thank you for your concern anyway.'

For a moment she looked reluctant to leave. For a moment she wanted to ask him what Daisy used to do, and why there was a bedroom in the cottage for someone who had never used it, why...

It wasn't the right time, or the right place. She gave him a quick hug, and hurried away.

Aidan shook his head, all too aware from her questioning eyes that the time was approaching when she would have to be told the truth.

All too aware she was the only other person in the world Daisy would be happy to tell it to.

− − −

Lord Finlay Finnegan clasped his hands together, and rested his chin on them. 'And why would you be thinking I even have a secret sideline, Rose?'

He spoke quietly, the Irish tint in his accent suddenly a little more prominent. Daisy knew the question was genuine enough, but was hiding a tinge of uncertainty, and designed to ask more than the one question the words would suggest.

'I might be a bit dotty, but I'm far more savvy than I appear, Finn.'

She used the shortened version of his name deliberately. A calculated risk, she was assuming it was only used by those within his secret inner circle. She saw his eyelids flicker slightly, and knew the risk had been worth it.

He sat back in the plush leather office chair, a slight smile on his lips. 'So Lady Rose... is that really who you are, or should I call you something else?'

She batted a hand in front of her face. 'Oh, silly boy. I'm not an undercover cop, or some kind of mole planted by your competitors. Trust me, if I was, this place would be swarming with people who want to end your life right now.'

He shook his head. 'So you really are Lady Rose Busch?'

'Of course I am. I have a website, you know. Go on, look it up...'

He tapped a few keys on the keypad, and studied the screen for a moment. 'Redrum House?'

'I know dear. For a while I made a living from tourists who thought Jack Nicholson lived there, or it was frequented by the ghost of a dead racehorse. But those days are gone now. And all those old windows are rotten, and so draughty.'

'So, if I may make so bold, what are you doing now, Rose?'

She dabbed a white handkerchief to her eye, deliberately. 'Sadly, not a lot, dear boy. And that dreadful habit of mine is so expensive, you know. Which is why I had to...diversify.'

'You? But you're...'

'Old? Don't let this wrinkly body fool you, young man. As I said, I'm not as dotty as I let people think.'

He leant forward again, his eyes suddenly narrowing into a suspicious stare. 'So would you be telling me Rose, that this is some kind of shakedown?'

'Dear boy! As if I would stoop to such lowlife tactics. Of course not.' She tried to look genuinely shocked. 'I'm here to offer you an... amalgamation.'

A slightly-disbelieving smile creased his face. 'Please forgive me, Rose, but I am struggling to accept this as genuine.'

'I see.' Daisy fumbled in the pocket of the tweed jacket. 'Perhaps this will assist in dispelling your disbelief.' She slapped a small clear plastic sealy-bag on the desk between his elbows.

He lifted it up, held it in front of his dark eyes. Then his brow puckered into a frown. He pulled apart the seal-strip, dipped a finger into the white powder inside, and touched it to his tongue.

'It's pure...' he whispered.

'Of course it is. It's from Jesse's stash.'

'Jesse... what... how..?'

Now Daisy had really got his attention. It was time to go in for the kill. She leant forward, made sure a stern and serious face was clear for him to see. 'Let's just say I am in possession of his stash now. But it's only one bag, which won't last long. Not in the circles I move in.'

He looked more than a little shocked. 'Did... did you kill him?'

'Don't be ridiculous. I thought you probably had.'

He shook his head. 'I don't kill people, Rose. Only if it's absolutely necessary. But if it wasn't you, then I know who likely did.'

'Who?'

'That's not for the here-and-now. I distance myself from everyone and everything below wholesale distributer level. But I still hear things.'

'And I hear that with Jesse's demise there's a hole in that distributer network now. Which is why I am here... to fill it. So, Lord Finlay Finnegan, are we in business?'

He lifted his hands in the air.' I suppose...'

'Good boy.'

Chapter 26

Daisy's host stood, and walked to the window, gazing out across his estate. For a moment her heart sank, but Sarah's face had gone. And judging by his lack of reaction, it was nowhere to be seen either.

He was silent for a moment, but then spoke in a quiet voice. 'I have little to do with the merchandise once I bring it into the country, Rose. My function is simply to supply the bulk, and what happens to it from then on is not my concern.'

'So how many wholesale distributers do you have, Finn?'

'Just the two... well, one now. Jesse and one other collect the packages from me, once a week, and that is the only connection I have to the rest of the operation. That way I have to deal with the minimum of people, and the minimum of risk. I prefer it that way.'

'And how do you get it into the country?'

He turned to face her. 'The less you know, the better. Let us just say my mother lives in Belgium... and the North Norfolk coast can be a somewhat wild and lonely place.'

'So do you visit your mother often?' Daisy asked a leading question.

He hesitated a moment. 'Once a week.'

'So where do I fit into this?'

'If I fit you into this, then you will take Jesse's place. But I am not sure someone like you has the necessary connections to make me sufficient money.'

Daisy walked over and joined him at the window. 'I've already demonstrated my fire-power, as it were. Do you not think the necessary connections are already in place?'

'I'm not sure. Jesse wholesaled to people who move in different circles to you.'

She laughed cynically. 'Oh yes, people who supply junkies who would sell their grandmother for a fix. Do you have any idea how many members of the English aristocracy are gagging for their highs, and have a lot more money to get them there? Trust me, the well-off are no less partial than the less well-off.'

'I suppose you are right. I have deliberately refrained from having anything to do with the habits of those I associate with. Can't trust them an aristocratic inch. But I confess I am intrigued by the fact you may be able to open up a whole new market for me, without me even being involved. If you have the connections you say you have.'

Daisy grinned, touched her nose. 'Oh son, you don't know the half of it. Have I not shown and told you enough? Let's get this line going, and then I can prove it.'

He turned away again, gazing out of the window at nothing in particular. It was a full minute before he answered, and Daisy knew he was churning over thoughts in his head, not all of them as positive as she would like.

It was the moment of truth. She'd done all she could, and now it was up to one simple decision that wasn't simple at all.

Finally he turned back to her. 'Give me your phone number. I leave for Belgium tomorrow, back Saturday. I will leave instructions where to meet me on my return. Those who distribute for me make just seven percent, but if you can handle the quantities involved, that is still a substantial income.'

'So I'm in then?'

'On a trial basis. Just please keep that AK-47 away from here in future.'

141

Daisy scribbled down her number, and then held out a deliberately-limp hand for him to shake. 'Jolly good. You won't regret it, dear boy. I'd better go now, and make a few arrangements. Toodlepip!'

As he watched her walk away, still looking a little bemused, she strode across the Persian rug as heavy-footed as she could, leaving a few more bits of dried mud in her wake, hoping it would annoy him just a little more.

She found Aidan on the forecourt, enjoying another Hamlet in the sunshine. His body visibly relaxed as he saw her.

'Oh, thank god...'

'Time to go, Henderson,' she said loudly, aware someone was probably watching. 'Drive me home, please.'

As soon as they were clear of the entrance and speeding along the road to home, Daisy let go of her alter-image and suddenly looked like a rag doll. Aidan glanced over. 'Dear, this is too much for you.'

'No it isn't. Not in this instance,' she snapped.

He shook his head in a despairing kind of way. 'I know this is a little too close to home for comfort, but even so...'

'Ok... so I'm emotionally drained. It's nothing a large brandy wouldn't cure. So put your foot down, and then I can have one.'

He put his foot down, knowing arguing was pointless. 'So did you get anything positive out of the ordeal?'

Finally she found a grin. 'Oh yes. I convinced him he couldn't do without me. So say hello to the new distributer to the aristocracy!'

Daisy swigged the brandy in one go, and poured another. There hadn't been a lot of conversation in the short drive home, Aidan all too aware Daisy had to take the time to bring her heart-rate down to a safe level. But there was one question she hadn't asked, which was always going to come.

'So what the hell was Sarah doing there? Did you know about that?'

'Of course not. I was the one who discovered her snooping at the window, fortunately. I sent her packing.'

'Silly girl. She could have jeopardised the whole sting.'

'Don't be too hard on her. Her intentions were good, she was just looking out for us.'

Daisy blinked away the sudden mistiness. 'I just couldn't bear for anything to happen to her...'

He put a gentle arm around her. 'She's still bringing back memories, huh?'

'Of course not... well maybe, a little. I failed to protect Celia... I can't fail again, dear.'

'I know, darling. But it isn't your responsibility to protect everyone.'

'Isn't it?'

'No, it isn't. Ok, we both welcomed Sarah into this, but she's a police officer. She knew what she was getting into.'

'Did she? We didn't even know how big this was when we first started digging up people's gardens. It was just the Times crossword then.'

He let out a chuckle, but there was little humour in it. 'That's true. But maybe it's time to tell the police what we know, and let them deal with it.'

'What, with no proof? They're not going to move against a fine, upstanding aristocrat on the word of a couple of raving old cronies. And Sarah's snooping saw nothing out of the ordinary. The one thing I did find out from my nerve-tingling conversation with my mark, was that he distances himself from most everything that could incriminate him. He's a respected member of the community, and he uses every drop of that status to make sure he's untouchable.'

'So how do little us bring him down?'

'There won't be a single shred of evidence at the manor, he makes sure of that. So we have to get proof another way. I'm his new distribution agent for a trial period, and in a very short time I'm to collect my first consignment. Catching him with his hands on the loot, to coin a phrase, is the only way to make anything stick.'

The lock of hair fell over Aidan's forehead as he shook his head. 'I was afraid you were going to say that.'

Chapter 27

Sarah turned up just after six, looking a little guilty. Daisy gave her a hug, and then narrowed her eyes as she handed her a glass of wine.

'Were you deliberately trying to put yourself in danger?'

'Like you weren't?'

'Well, ok. But it was necessary.'

'Necessary? So what is your definition of necessary, Daisy?'

The question made her lower her head, talk to the floor. 'When you've been through what we have Sarah, bringing down Finn is necessary, trust me.'

'You might need to explain that a little more. And what were the antics with the AK-47 all about, anyway?'

'Making a point. A point he couldn't ignore. And as for explaining things... can we eat first? It's just a simple Bolognese, but Aidan makes it special.'

'An added portion of pepperoni,' he grinned as he gave the brew a final stir, and then carried it to the table. Daisy drizzled some olive oil over the pasta, and then sat down beside him.

'Talking of necessary, I found out some stuff today that makes me certain catching him red-handed is the only way to bring him down.'

'You should let the police deal with it, Daisy.'

'Police? All due respect, Sarah, but he's untouchable. There's no connection between him and his network. The only way is to bring an end to his activities at source, to coin a phrase. Stop the supply chain before it even begins.'

'And that's down to us?'

'No. Aidan and me, dear. You're not involved, not when it's this big.'

Sarah put down her fork, and gaped open-mouthed at Daisy. 'You've got to be kidding. I risked my safety today, on my day off, to make sure you were okay, and now you're telling me I'm not part of the sting?'

Daisy put a hand on her arm. 'Yes dear, and that's precisely why I don't want you involved. Your carelessness today almost ruined the whole thing, and... and I don't want you making such mistakes again, when the stakes are at their highest.'

Aidan put it in basic terms. 'Daisy and me don't want you getting harmed... or worse.'

Sarah nodded, slotting one or two jigsaw pieces into place. Then she asked a leading question, which had nothing to do with the operation. 'Whose room is that upstairs, guys?'

Aidan's eyes dropped to the table, but Daisy reached for her wine and took a sip. 'I keep it for Celia, our daughter.'

Sarah saw the mistiness in her eyes. 'And where is Celia, Daisy?'

She opened her mouth to answer, but something stopped the words coming out. A Nokia phone sitting on the worktop, which must have been ten years old, started to jingle out the tones of Rule Britannia. Daisy looked at Aidan, a little shocked. 'That's an ancient phone I gave him the number for. So it can only be one person calling.'

She walked quickly to the island unit, grabbed the phone and answered as she flicked it to speaker. 'Yes, hello? Lady Rose Busch here.'

The voice on the other end sounded jolly, confident. The faint Irish tint didn't seem to be so much of a tint now. 'Top of the evening to you, Rose. And how are you, may I ask?'

'I'm still on board, if that's what you're implying, Finn.'

'Not at all, Rose. But talking of on board, I was wondering if you would be up for a little trip in the morning?'

'Trip?'

'I got to thinking after you left, as we're planning to be partners now, you might like to accompany me on my trip to... see my mother tomorrow. Understand how the land lies, you might say.'

'The land in Belgium?'

'Yes indeed. I have a boat at Wells. Would you be liking a little voyage, Rose?'

'I'm humbled, dear boy. And a little surprised. I thought you preferred to keep such things... in the family.'

They heard him sigh. 'Normally I do. But as our little liaison could bloom and flourish into something much bigger, I was thinking you might like to meet my mother.'

Daisy saw Aidan throw his hands in the air, but ignored his gesture. 'I think I would like that, Finn.'

'Good. I will confess though, there is another reason. We'll be taking two boats over tomorrow, and I could do with a little extra crew. So please bring your man with you.'

'Henderson goes everywhere with me anyway. So yes, we'll be there. What time do we leave?'

'Early. Could you be getting yourselves there for eight in the morning, when the tide conditions are favourable? My boat is on the pontoon just to the west of the town harbour. I'll meet you on the landing stage. Everything is on board, so just bring a toothbrush!'

Again she ignored Aidan's shake of the head. 'We'll be there, Finn.'

'Splendid. I'll be looking forward to seeing you.'

The phone clicked off. Daisy glanced over to Aidan and Sarah, knowing one of them would say something. Both of them did.

'It sounds like a trap to me.'

'You really are a dozy old biddie after all.'

Daisy found a smile, although it came out as a humourless one. 'Oh, you two of little faith. He just wants to make sure I'm loyal to the cause.'

Aidan repeated himself. 'It's a trap.'

Daisy glared at him. 'What if it is? He'd already told me he was going to Belgium tomorrow. He's going to be bringing back a consignment, whatever else happens. We just have to be prepared for the unexpected.'

'I wish I had your flippant attitude to danger,' Sarah groaned.

'Flippant? Oh my dear, you have no idea. Finn and the packages are going to be in the same place. It's the golden opportunity to catch him at it.'

'Talking of packages...'

Daisy grabbed the two bags of flour from the bread bin, slapped them on the table in front of Sarah. 'Yes dear, I suggest you hand these over to your boss in the morning. I apologise for one of them having a slight puncture in it. I had to...commandeer a tiny bit, to make sure Finn knew I was for real.'

'Daisy...'

'Now, if you wouldn't mind leaving us, dear. Henderson and I have a crack-of-dawn start in the morning, so I think an early night is called for. We'll be in touch when we need you!'

Sarah found herself virtually bundled out of the door, the two bags of very valuable flour hastily thrown into a

148

Waitrose carrier bag. As she drove away, she knew why Daisy had been so brusque with her. She was doing all she could to protect her from danger.

But she'd made one mistake. The phone was on speaker so Aidan could hear the conversation with Finn. The conversation that included the time they were setting off.

Constable Sarah Lowry had no intention of keeping out of danger. She also knew the Norfolk police wouldn't do anything to stop a well-respected aristocrat from taking a cruise to visit his mother.

Daisy and Aidan needed protecting from themselves, again. Finn needed to be brought down too, but Daisy was right. He could only get his just desserts if he was caught with the merchandise in his hands.

It was an impossible situation, which was only going to have a positive outcome if all three of them put themselves in the middle of that impossible situation. By walking willingly into a dangerous endgame all three of them knew was a raging certainty.

As far as Sarah was concerned, Daisy, Aidan and she were a team, for better or for worse.

Whether the rest of the team liked it or not.

Chapter 28

Aidan looked his wife over as she strode into the kitchen area. 'I have to say, ma'am, you look every bit the dotty aristocrat dressed for a voyage to the North Pole.'

'Thank you, Henderson. I shall take that as one of your many compliments.'

He shook his head, watching her closely as she flicked on the kettle and grabbed the mugs. It was six-thirty on a beautiful late-summer morning, and his pseudo-aristocrat was dressed for the occasion... if it had been midwinter.

A thick grey fisherman's jumper sat over equally-thick dark-coloured, old-fashioned trousers, their bottoms tucked into the now-famous pink flowered wellington boots. A wide-brimmed, waterproof man's hat dominated her head, her silver curls bunned tight beneath it.

She saw him watching. 'It'll be cold out on the water,' she said coyly.

'Better go fetch my sou'wester then,' he retorted.

She handed him a mug of creamed coffee. 'Drink this and quit being so insolent, servant.'

'Yes ma'am. You never did tell me what your last servant died of.'

'Terminal exhaustion. Now get your boots on, it'll be time to go in a minute.'

'It's only a fifteen-mile trip, dear. Plenty of time to enjoy our coffee first.'

She opened her mouth to say something that might have given away the fact she was more than a little nervous, but didn't get the chance. From outside, the crunch of tyres on gravel made them both shake their heads.

'No prizes for guessing who that is.'

They both sat quietly on the stools next to the island unit, waiting for the smiling face to appear in the kitchen doorway. A minute later it did.

'Hi guys!'

'Go away.'

'Nice to see you too, Daisy.'

'I told you we don't want you here.'

'Sorry, official police business. Any of that coffee left?'

'So where's your official-police-business uniform?'

'I'm undercover.'

'Really.'

'Well, kind of.'

'I don't believe you.'

Sarah sat down on the third stool, sipping her stolen coffee and still grinning. 'Tough. It's the duty of the Norfolk police force to ensure the safety of their elderly residents, no matter how much they've lost their minds.'

Aidan shook his head for the tenth time that morning. 'So now she not only gate-crashes a private party, she insults us as well.'

'I don't know what the world is coming to,' said Daisy.

'Ok, just stop it. You two might be doing something that's one step from insanity, but you're not doing it alone. I'm coming with you, whether you like it or not.'

'And I suppose if we say no, you'll just follow us in your car.'

'You got that one right.'

'Damn speakerphones,' said Daisy.

'We could hide her car keys.'

'Or I could get my gun out...'

'Ok, I said stop it... I considered arresting you for endangering your own lives, but I'm not going to. I'd never

151

hear the last of it if I did... from you or Burrows. So the only alternative is to see this through with you.'

'There is another alternative. Go home right now, and wait until tomorrow when we call Burrows as soon as we know the location of the merchandise drop, 'cos I doubt it will be back at Wells. It'll be somewhere else on the Norfolk coast, more remote.'

'Sorry. Not going home.'

Daisy glanced to Aidan, who was all too aware of the reason for the glance. Sarah reminded them both even more of Celia, when she was being stubborn. 'Sarah... oh, what's the point?'

'No point at all. As far as Finn is concerned I'm your daughter, Lady Rose. Just along for the ride...oh, I'm sorry if that strikes a raw nerve...'

Daisy's eyes dropped to the mug in her lap. Going on real-life events, Sarah could easily pass as her daughter. The daughter she wouldn't intentionally expose to danger.

But Sarah was right, and she and Aidan had no choice. She'd put the phone on speaker when Finn had called the previous evening, not expecting him to say what he did, and certainly not anticipating the time and the place would be broadcast for all to hear.

'You're a pain in my butt, Sarah Lowry.'

The grin got wider. 'I know. But I do have a plan.'

'Really. What plan?'

'Well, as we're walking into a scenario without escape routes, it's best that the less you know, the better. I'll keep it to myself for if and when it's needed, if you don't mind.'

A half-hour later, the two older members of the party climbed reluctantly into the BMW, in the company of their younger, more excited companion.

Two minutes later they were speeding along the Norfolk country lanes in the direction of the market town of Fakenham, all three of them knowing there was little choice but to head into a scenario without any obvious escape routes, which just might turn out to be a trap.

Chapter 29

'Well, Lady Rose, and who might this delightful vision of loveliness be?'

Lord Finlay Finnegan looked extremely pleased and rather suspicious both at the same time, as he took the young hand of the pretty girl he hadn't seen before, and kissed her fingers in a very formal, aristocratic way.

Daisy didn't give Sarah chance to answer. 'This is my lovely daughter, C... Sarah. She's my business manager, and she's fully briefed in everything I do. And you can keep your paws off her too.'

He looked suitably offended. 'Rose... I shall consider that an insult born out of parental but misguided protection. As if I would. Um... you haven't brought that automatic rifle, have you?'

She grinned as menacingly as she could. 'Safely locked away in the gun cabinet at Redrum House, Finn. But I don't need bullets to protect my daughter.'

His eyes narrowed. 'I'm sure you don't, Rose. No matter, the more the merrier! What do you think?'

He glanced to the very expensive luxury white cruiser moored to the pontoon next to them. Daisy cast her eyes over its sleek modern shape and the dark elegantly-shaped windows. About sixty feet long, its twin diesels were already growling quietly away, spewing cooling water from the exhausts at the stern.

A rear teak-lined deck bigger than her patio at the cottage looked like it had built-in seating for at least twenty people, and a cooking point integrated into the side for al fresco meals in the Mediterranean sunshine.

A flying bridge partly formed a roof over the deck, and although she couldn't see it, Daisy knew it would run most of the way over the raised stateroom too, and would contain more luxurious seating and chilled drink dispensers, so those enjoying the spectacular view from its high-level vantage point didn't have to climb down to the deck for refreshments.

It must have set the good lord back at least a couple of million pounds. Or the equivalent in lira, because the luxury cruiser had a distinctly Italian look about it.

'Very impressive,' she breathed, trying to look awestruck at the spoils of his secret sideline. 'Can't wait to experience its pleasures for myself.'

'Ah... well, Rose, I'm afraid that will have to wait for the return journey tomorrow.'

'It will?'

He put a hand on her arm. 'Come, let me show you your vessel for the outward passage.'

He led them gently but firmly further along the pontoon, to where a slightly-smaller vessel had almost been obscured by the bulk of the shiny white fibreglass of his pride and joy.

This one was growling away too, a single Cummins diesel spluttering out exhaust water from a black-painted, rounded stern. It wasn't fibreglass, and it wasn't new.

It looked like a fishing trawler, but the cabin and wheelhouse surrounded by its traditional wooden deck looked a lot newer than its old wooden hull. Its main mast and the smaller one on its stern looked like they were just as old as its ancient hull, supported by what seemed like miles of old rope rigging.

Finn smiled as he held out a hand to its traditional splendour. 'It belongs to my mother. We are taking it back

155

to her home near Antwerp. Do not fear though, Rose. It is a converted crabbing boat, and is very comfortable inside.'

'You want us to drive her?'

As Daisy said that, she caught sight of a slightly-familiar figure emerging from the wheelhouse, and realised that Finn definitely didn't want them to drive it. Their genial host confirmed it. 'No, no. Johnson there will helm it. But, whilst my very modern vessel virtually drives itself, this crabber does not, and so if you will be so kind to accompany Johnson, he will be grateful for the help. Then we can all return on my boat tomorrow, together with the... merchandise.'

'I do like a traditional boat,' said Daisy, a little reluctantly.

'Good. We will cruise both boats together today, and then take evening dinner on my boat tonight. Now it is time to leave, so if you will be kind enough to board, we can depart.'

Their host was right about one thing; the crabber had been converted very nicely. Daisy and Aidan threw their overnight bags down onto the double bunk of the main cabin, and glanced around. Everything was varnished mahogany and white painted walls, apart from the two large portholes which were new, and shiny brass.

A modern duvet sat inside a thick cover that looked more like a tapestry, and a patterned red carpet covered what there was of the floor. A shiny wooden door led to a small en suite, containing a miniature shower, basin and toilet. Brass oil lamps that were not oil lamps at all adorned the mahogany walls, and a small flat-screen TV sat on the traditional dressing table, and totally spoiled the feeling they'd stepped back into a bygone era.

'Very cosy,' mused Aidan, not at all convincingly.

Daisy was about to reply that it actually was, but the note of the diesel engine rose a little, and the gruff tones of Finn's Vinnie-Jones lookalike butler called down.

'Could do with someone casting off, if you wouldn't mind.'

Daisy and Aidan walked through into the companionway, just as Sarah emerged from an equally-cosy smaller cabin. Together they headed onto the spacious deck. Finn's luxury cruiser was just passing them, the man himself high up on the flybridge helm, waving cheerily as he saw them.

Aidan headed to the bow, began to undo the forward rope, and Sarah did the same for the stern rope. In the wheelhouse, Johnson was playing with two tiny joysticks, and as his crew jumped back aboard, the old boat moved sideways away from the pontoon, the newly-fitted bow and stern-thrusters kicking in to clear them from any obstructions.

In mid-channel, with the salt-marsh sandbanks on their right and the town on their left, one of his hands flicked to the main throttle lever and the other grasped the traditional ships wheel. The old crabber began to move forward, following in the wake of the white cruiser up ahead.

The three crew members stood together on the deck, watching the concrete quayside and the buildings of the town dwindle to specks as they followed the narrow deep channel marked by buoys. They passed the multitude of smaller boats on swinging moorings, heading for the beach proper a half-mile from the town, protected by salt-marshes from the vastness of the North Sea.

Daisy and Aidan looked at each other. Being gently but forcibly shepherded onto the second boat didn't exactly make for peace of mind. But someone else was grinning from ear to ear as the salty wind sliced through her blonde hair.

'This is so exciting!' she said.

Chapter 30

The three of them stood on the deck, taking in the clean fresh air of North Norfolk, one of them apparently enjoying the experience more than the others. The roofs of the caravans lined up in the holiday park to their left came and went, and then the beach proper was in view.

One or two morning dog-walkers waved as they passed by, the boat keeping to the deep channel. Then, suddenly, civilisation was behind them. As the two boats navigated the marked channel between the sandbanks, the wide expanse of the ocean proper was right in front of them, less than a half-mile away.

Daisy glanced back, her eyes following the wake of the crabber as it fanned out across the calm water behind them. She swallowed hard, felt Aidan's arm around her waist, and knew he was thinking the same thing.

In two minutes time, the last remnants of solid ground would be out of view. And so would any shred of a safety net. They were at the mercy of their lord and master, and it wasn't a comforting place to be.

'Let's go below,' she said to the others. 'Time for a conflab.'

As they climbed down to the rear well, and through the door that led to the sleeping cabins, the last of the sandbanks passed to their right. They'd reached the expanse of the North Sea, and in just a few minutes time, there wouldn't even be a sandbank left to see.

The three of them sat in a line on the double bunk. Daisy was the first to speak. 'So, for the sake of argument, let's assume this is all on the level, and after we deliver the boat to Finn's mum, we all head back to England tomorrow in opulent luxury, together with the latest consignment.'

'I still think it's a trap,' said Aidan despondently.

Daisy couldn't disagree with him, no matter how much she would have liked to. 'You may be right, dear. We just have to be vigilant, even though we don't have many cards to play.'

'There's only Vinnie Jones on board, and three of us. We could mutiny, take over this boat.'

'And then what? Finn would realise what we'd done, open his throttles and leave us to pootle home, and still go to pick up his consignment. Then all my pretence will have been in vain, and we've got nothing to show for it.'

'Except our lives.'

'Well yes, there is that, dear. But you're assuming this isn't on the level. I was pretty convincing, if I say so myself, and Finn saw the opportunities I shoved in front of his face.'

Sarah spoke for the first time. 'So what is the plan, Daisy? If we all get to head home with the consignment, what then?'

'I shall use my feminine and slightly-dotty charm to try and find out where the drop point is, before we actually get there. Then it's a simple job to call your boss, and get him and the drugs squad to meet us there... and hey ho, Finn is caught red-handed.'

'Sounds simple when you put it like that,' Aidan groaned.

Daisy's head lowered. 'It is simple, Dip. And the longer I think about it, the more I think it may be too simple.'

He slipped an arm around her shoulders. 'Hey, Flower... the best things in life are simple, are they not? If Finn's greed is powerful enough, that will help convince him you're on the level. If that's the case, then we're home and dry... rather literally.'

'I can't help thinking he's going to test me somehow.'

'Maybe he will. And you'll pass with flying colours. And anyway, as you have no doubt realised, it's too late now.'

'Thanks for that, dear. And please stop with the nautical references.'

'Sorry, dear. But we are sailing quite close to the wind.' He caught the glare, turned to Sarah. 'So, Constable Sarah Lowry, what's your secret plan?'

'I... um, no. Sorry, all I can say is it's a back-up plan, if things go wrong. Given the current situation, it's maybe better you don't know.'

'Sarah? There's only Johnson aboard, and he's busy sailing the thing.'

'I don't mean... if things turn nasty, I'll tell you then.'

'Dear, she doesn't want us to know, in case things do go west and Finn forces it out of us.'

'Oh, I see. But we're heading east...'

'Funny guy.'

Things didn't go west for the next few hours. The boats, in line astern, continued to cruise east, and all was exactly as it should be. In the lead boat, Finn had headed for open water, and they could see nothing on any horizon but sea.

Johnson 'Vinnie Jones' the butler was dutifully following a couple of hundred metres behind. The sea was relatively calm, and a warm sun beat down from a sky peppered with small white cumulus clouds.

It was a beautiful, peaceful day on the North Sea.

Aidan made coffees at the propane stove in the small galley, and took one to Johnson at the helm. He grunted a gruff thank you, and carried on following his boss's wake. Standing in the rear well, his three passengers sipped their coffees, watching the grey-blue water that was the only thing filling their view.

'Well, we're way out to sea now,' mused Daisy. 'If we could see the shore, we'd probably be looking at Lowestoft.'

It was hardly a brilliant piece of detective work. On the hazy horizon, the gently-rotating vanes of a hundred wind generators were glinting in the sun, and as the miles clicked off, the bulk of two or three oil rigs came into sight.

But then even they were gone, and all they could see in every direction was the gently-rolling sea. They were leaving the green fields of England well behind, and 'open water' took on a new meaning. It was mid-afternoon, and none of them needed to be experienced seafarers to work out they were halfway between England and Belgium.

Sarah seemed to be suffering from Daisy's itchy feet. 'I'm going to explore,' she announced. 'If something is going to happen, I need to know every inch of this ship.'

'Boat,' said Aidan.

'Whatever. See you in a bit.' She disappeared through the narrow varnished double doors. Daisy looked at Aidan. 'There's not much to see. Three cabins below deck, a couple of toilets... the rest is chain lockers and storage, I guess.'

'She needs to do something. Sarah clearly thinks the worst is going to happen, so she wants to be ready.'

'She's a police officer. They always think the worst is going to happen.'

'Don't you?'

She couldn't sound that convincing. 'Not until we get to Antwerp. That's when we might need to be extra-vigilant.'

'We're out of UK waters now, though.'

'Did you have to say that?'

Maybe Aidan had a premonition, maybe it was just an idle observation. But ten minutes later, when Sarah's frantic head appeared at the doorway, they both knew straightaway all was not well.

'You'd better come below, guys. I've just found something.'

They followed her into their cabin, and she closed the door quickly behind them. There was a piece of paper in her hand; it looked like some kind of receipt.

'I nosed around in the third cabin. Seems like Johnson is using it, his bag was sitting on the bunk. And so was this...'

Daisy and Aidan looked over the piece of paper. It was a receipt...

THE WELLS LUXURY BOAT COMPANY

Luxury Boat Hire for Fishing Trips

And then underneath, the words that stabbed the sharpest dagger in the world into their hearts...

Hired to Mrs. Daisy Morrow and Mr. Aidan Henderson, the vessel 'Princess of Wells', for the period of Friday 27th to Sunday 29th August.

It went on to list out prices and conditions of hire, and ended with a few simple instructions for picking up the vessel, which Finn had clearly done on their behalf before they arrived.

They didn't bother to read much of that.

Daisy shook her head. 'So Finn's mother doesn't own this boat after all.'

163

Aidan glared at her with a disbelieving expression on his face. 'You've just read what I've read, and that's all you can say?'

Chapter 31

'Calm down, dear. We just have to think logically, and find a way out.'

'A way out?' So you can walk on water then? Or sprout wings and fly us all back to England like Tinkerbelle?'

She tapped him lovingly on the arm. 'We might have our very own Captain Hook dear, but I'm sure we can be like Peter Pan and outsmart him.'

'How? This isn't a Disney film.'

'But there's a dinghy on davits at the stern.'

Sarah tried to be more practical. 'Ok, let's think this through. Daisy, you obviously didn't fool Finn like you believed.'

'I thought I'd given an Oscar-winning performance. How the hell did he see through it so quickly?'

'No idea, but he did. And now he's making sure you won't be able to ruin his little sideline. But I still don't get the point of hiring this boat in your real names.'

'Oh dear.'

'Oh dear?' gasped Aidan.

'I'm so sorry, you two. It seems like I've really put my foot in it this time.'

'Yes, you have. But I still don't see...'

Daisy lowered her head, spoke quietly. 'It's obvious when you look at it from Finn's perspective. Somehow he was on to us from the off, and he also knew we were a substantial threat to his operation. So he had to get rid of us, but make it seem like it was all perfectly innocent.'

Sarah turned away, and cast her suddenly-seeing eyes to the roof. 'He hired this boat in your names, making it seem like you'd decided on a weekend sea-fishing trip. Then, somehow you manage to get into difficulties, and end up losing your lives. An unfortunate accident at sea.'

'And if he says the right things, like he left us part way to carry on to Belgium to see his mother, no one is any the wiser.'

Aidan groaned out his usual expletive when things had gone wrong. 'Bugger.'

'Yes dear, bugger. Any time soon I suspect we will be getting wet feet. This is an old wooden boat. It's not inconceivable it could spring a hull plank.'

'And we'll walk the plank.'

'We won't need to, Dip. The ocean will come to meet us, not the other way round.'

'Bugger.'

Sarah was shaking her head, like there was more than one defeat at stake. 'I don't believe this... drowning at sea is bad enough, but Finn is not only going to get away with murder, but laugh all the way to Belgium and pick up his stash a totally free man.'

'Precisely. If we don't do something, this will all have been in vain.'

Aidan shook his head, a double lock of silver hair flopping over his forehead. 'Are you two listening to yourselves? Sod the sting... we're about to lose our lives.'

He turned away. Daisy wrapped her arms around his waist and hugged him tightly. 'Dear, I'm sorry I dragged you into this. It was selfish of me. I was quite prepared to go down as long as Finn got his comeuppance... but now it seems I won't even have that satisfaction.'

He spun round, and kissed her softly. 'You listen to me... no one's going down, even if that is an unfortunate turn of phrase. We need to go and overpower Vinnie Jones, turn this boat around, and head back to England. Then... then maybe we can get Finn a different way.'

Daisy smiled, lovingly but sadly. 'Dear, your chivalry is admirable, but that won't work. Even if we manage to throw Johnson to the sharks, that plastic rocket of Finns will soon catch up with us. We're no match for his twin diesels.'

'Then... then we'll call the coastguard or something. He won't dare interfere with us then.'

'And all they'll find is an empty express cruiser. No packages, nothing to incriminate him. Again.'

'Daisy dear, at least we'll be alive. Is catching him red-handed really more important than that?'

It was Sarah who answered. 'Aidan, we've come this far. Correct me if I'm wrong, but from Daisy's point of view, Finn's main source of income is from something that runs very close to her heart?'

'You're not wrong there, Sarah dear,' said Daisy.

'Maybe one day you'll tell me what happened, but for now... well, we have to do all we can to terminate this evil. Daisy is right, the only way is to catch him red-handed. You two have had your cover blown, but maybe I haven't. But if I have or haven't, it doesn't matter. There might be a way to make sure we get him.'

Daisy pricked up her ears, but it was Aidan who frowned to her. 'And what way might that be?'

Sarah tapped her wrist. 'Fitbit!'

Chapter 32

'What?'

'Fitbit!' Sarah was still showing them her wrist.

'Oh come on, Dip,' said Daisy, a smile on her face. 'You're more tech-savvy than I am.'

'I know what a Fitbit is... well, kind of. But how does it help us?'

'It's the latest generation, a Charge Four. My father bought it for me last Christmas. It's got GPS built in!'

'I still don't see how...'

'Ok, confession time. When I went home last night, I told my father everything. He's ex-force, remember? At first he freaked out, but after he calmed down I told him what my plan B was, and he reluctantly agreed with me that we had to catch Finn in the act. I left my phone with him, which is linked to the Fitbit.'

'But surely we're out of range now?'

'We are now, but when Finn gets back to wherever he's going to offload the packages, this Fitbit will be in range, and my father will be watching the screen on my phone. The only issue is that somehow I have to get this device onto Finn's boat without him knowing it's there. Then we don't have to be on board ourselves, because the Fitbit will automatically GPS his movements as soon as he gets close to the North Norfolk coast. It wasn't quite what I had in mind, but it is a solution.'

Daisy glanced to Aidan, who nodded very slightly again, and turned away. She pulled Sarah onto the bunk by her side. 'It's a good plan, dear. Except for one thing. Somehow, we have to get the Fitbit and you onto Finn's boat without him knowing.'

She looked horrified. 'Daisy, I'm not leaving you two. Not for anything.'

'Yes, you are. Aidan and me are in our twilight years, you have your whole life to live. If there's the slightest chance you can survive this, we have to take it.'

'And what about you two? I can't just abandon you.'

'Oh, you can. And anyway, all is not lost. I brought a second phone, and it's hidden somewhere Finn will never find it.'

'You're just saying that to make me feel better.'

'No Sarah. On... on my real daughter's life, I swear I'm telling the truth.'

Sarah stared into her eyes, and then nodded sadly. 'Ok, you wouldn't say that just for effect. But how do I get on board Finn's boat without being seen?'

'Let me think.' Daisy went into vacant-eyed thinking mode. The room went silent for a full minute. Then she slapped Aidan's thigh. 'There's only one way. But you might get a little damp.'

'Getting wet is the least of the issues.'

'There's a massive bathing platform at the stern of Finn's boat. It's at a much lower level than the rear deck. He can't see that from the flybridge. But he'll have to come alongside to get Johnson on board. The rear well on this boat is a lower level too, and shielded to some extent by the cabin top. If you can clamber onto his bathing platform from our well, you might not be seen. But when he gets under way, the bathing platform might get a little wet, just above water level as it is. But I think it's the only route.'

'But they'll notice I'm not on board, surely?'

Aidan grinned. 'It's got to be timed perfectly, right at the last moment. Odds on they'll scupper this boat and leave us to drown. If we create some kind of diversion to keep their

169

minds off you, you might just be able to slip away unnoticed. It has to be worth a try.'

'I don't like it.'

Daisy pulled her into a hug. 'Neither do we, Sarah. But do you have a better idea?'

Her eyes lowered to her slender hands, suddenly wringing together in her lap. 'No, I don't,' she whispered.

'Ok. It's down to you now, Sarah. No matter what happens to Aidan and me, you're the only one who can bring about endgame now. Don't let me down.'

Sarah wiped away a tear. 'I can't believe it's come to this.'

'Oh, have faith. When we see you disappear over the horizon, we can call someone. We can't be too far from the European coast now, so we'll be rescued.'

Sarah nodded. It was blatantly obvious Daisy was saying the words without any conviction behind them. They were a long way from either coast, that much was clear enough. Finn wasn't going to scupper their boat if there was any real chance of rescue. Risking a charge of attempted murder was the last thing he was going to do.

But she knew Daisy was saying the words as much for her own benefit as hers. Deep down she knew the chances of getting through to anyone who could rescue them in the time they'd have were remote, to say the least. But sending her young friend on her way with a smile, and a strong hope in her heart there would be some kind of rescue, was something Daisy clearly felt she had to do.

To make sure she would actually leave at all.

So she smiled back to the silver-haired lady who was doing all she could to make her feel better, still unsure if when it came to it, she actually would go. But she knew that where they were right then, the Fitbit GPS was useless, and all she would achieve from staying would be to lose her life along with her friends'.

She didn't get any longer to make a final decision. The engine note changed, as the powerful diesel was throttled back. Then they heard a couple of short bursts, as Johnson manoeuvred the boat closer to Captain Hook's.

Then the engine fell quiet, the throttle pushed to neutral. They felt the clunk as the two boats came together, and then all was quiet for a minute.

Daisy glanced nervously to Aidan, who took her hand, and then slipped the other into Sarah's. She saw him smile in a petrified kind of way, doing his best to hide his fear. 'I think it's time,' he said slowly to them both.

'Don't let me down,' said Daisy, almost glaring evils at Sarah.

And then the cabin door flew open, and the smiling face of Captain Hook was grinning a triumphant smirk at them.

'So there you are.'

Chapter 33

'And there you are,' said Daisy, matching his smile even though it was the last thing she felt like doing. 'So nice of you to pop over and make sure we were well.'

He ignored the sarcasm. ''Tis a terrible thing I have to be doing now,' he said, his eyes flicking to the receipt sitting on the bunk. 'But I'm sure you understand why it has to be done.'

'I don't suppose telling you we won't say a word is going to cut it?'

He shook his head, still grinning. 'Not at all, Mrs. Morrow.'

'It's Miss.'

'Whatever.' He glanced to Sarah. 'And such a tragic shame... a young and pretty thing like she is too.'

'Just spare her, Finn. Please? She's got nothing to do with this. She only came along for the ride. She knows better than to incur your wrath... don't you, Sarah?'

She nodded in a frightened kind of way, partly for his benefit, partly because she really was terrified. But Finn looked unmoved. 'We really should leave you in peace now. Important things to do, you know.'

'I can't believe you sussed me out so quickly. I must be losing my touch.'

He laughed. 'Indeed, Daisy my dear. But I will confess you almost had me fooled. It was only your eagerness to make your mark, as you might say, which gave you away.'

'I don't understand.'

They heard movement in the walkway behind their smiling host, and then a face appeared over his shoulder. A black face, topped by a red, green and yellow beanie hat. It was grinning too, its owner safe in the knowledge that this time he really was untouchable.

'Hello, Desmond.'

The grin faded. 'It's Des.'

'Aidan could do with a haircut, if you can spare the time.'

Suddenly he looked agitated, itching to use his knife without getting shot. But Finn was in his way, standing in the narrow doorway. 'Now Des... don't let her acid tongue spoil things. How would it look when they fish out her body and find stab wounds?'

He shook his head to the left, then to the right, still itching to inflict pain. 'You the boss,' he said, extremely reluctantly.

'Yes, I am. Now go do what I asked, please.'

Finn stood aside, deliberately, and for the first time they could see Desmond had a twelve-pound sledgehammer in his hands. 'You's gettin' what's comin' to you, lady bitch!' he growled venomously.

'Calm down, Des. There's an oversized chain locker in the bow, where the hull planks are visible. One of those will suffice. Just separate it from the rest, ok? Not too much obvious damage.'

Desmond grinned with a menacing kind of joy at the task he'd been given, silently stabbed an accusing finger at Daisy, and disappeared.

Finn shook his head. 'Do forgive Des. He's a little edgy, but a useful employee at times like these. And he was invaluable at unmasking your sting, Daisy.'

'How so?'

'Des has a room in the servant's quarters at the manor. He would likely not have even seen you the day you came. If not for one thing.'

'One thing?'

173

'Your little shooting display, the noise from which likely caught the attention of half the population of West Norfolk. The poor boy is still a little traumatised by your automatic rifle, so perhaps understandably he went to see what was going on. When he saw who it was on the other end of it... well, the rest is history.'

'Poor boy,' said Daisy.

The dull clunk of sledgehammer on hull drifted through the doorway. Five thumps later it stopped, and a minute after that the tall, skinny figure holding it passed by, heading for the deck. He still couldn't help stabbing a triumphant finger at Daisy before he was out of sight. Then Johnson appeared behind his boss. 'All done,' he said gruffly.

'Oh guys, please give Johnson your phones.'

Aidan handed over his, and Daisy did the same, giving up her shiny new Galaxy. 'Sarah didn't bring hers,' she said.

'Really,' the butler replied disbelievingly. Then he frisked her, and did the same to Daisy and Aidan, just to make sure. Then he moved quickly, ransacking the overnight bags in case there were any communication devices in them. Then he did the same in the other two cabins, even though one of them was his.

'No more phones,' he reported to his boss two minutes later.

'Throw them overboard, please.'

'Are we allowed to watch our demise from the deck?' said Aidan.

Finn turned away. 'Please, feel free. Enjoy your last breaths of air in the sunshine!'

'I'm going to hooey,' Sarah cried, putting a hand across her mouth, and brushing past Finn on her way to the toilet nearer the stern of the boat.

He looked genuinely sad. 'Such a shame,' he muttered, like he really meant it.

'Won't stop you though, will it?' Daisy spat out.

'Sadly, no it won't,' he called back as he headed to the deck. Daisy and Aidan followed him. As soon as they made the open air they could see the dinghy. It wasn't on its davits anymore. Drifting further away with every second, it was already two hundred yards from the boat, bobbing away on the gentle waves.

Captain Hook and his two pirates looked like they were heading for their ship. Unable to see where Sarah was, Daisy knew there was nothing else for it, glanced to Aidan and nodded. Together they screamed as loudly as they could, and launched themselves at their boarders.

They didn't stand a hope in hell of course, but that wasn't the point. Aidan managed to get his hands around Johnson's neck. Daisy shoved Desmond as hard as she could. He lost his balance, fell to the deck, and Daisy dropped onto him heavily. But then he pulled his knife, so she backed away. Aidan let go of Johnson's neck and backed away too, as he whipped out a handgun and brandished it at him.

Finn, already halfway up the ladder to the flybridge, called out. 'Children... don't do anything incriminating, that's what they'd like.' Then he laughed, infuriatingly. 'Really, you two?'

'Last chance saloon, and all that,' said Daisy as she picked herself up from the deck.

'Fair enough, Calamity Jane,' he chuckled. 'I suppose I can understand you trying the impossible. Well, see ya'. Not.'

He made the flybridge, checked that his henchmen were aboard, and then gave a cheery wave as he sat himself

175

down at the upper helm. The engines growled in response to the throttle being shoved forward a little, and the space between the two boats grew bigger.

And Desmond, standing on the side deck halfway along, finally smiled as he held a single finger up at the pensioner who had frightened the hell out of him a few days before.

'Did Sarah make it?' said Daisy.

'We'll know in a second,' said Aidan, as he put an arm around her waist.

The big white floating machine, the waves reflecting off its shiny hull, moved slowly away from the leaky hull of the old crabber. When the boats were twenty feet apart, Finn shoved the throttles to full, and as the bow pointed into the air and the throaty roar of the engines filled their ears, it sped quickly away, Desmond's single finger still pointing into the air.

And then they could see the bathing platform, and the tiny figure sitting right up against the stern transom with her arms around her knees, so she couldn't be seen from the rest of the boat.

She lifted a forlorn hand, a silent, poignant wave of goodbye that spoke a thousand words about the way she was feeling. And Daisy burst into tears, buried her face in Aidan's shoulder.

'Now I don't know which one of us is in most danger,' she sobbed.

Chapter 34

Sarah allowed a few tears to fall, as she sat on the bathing platform with her knees up to her chin, watching the wake fanning out behind the boat as it sped at high speed towards its destination.

It wasn't the fact she'd lied to her boss, or that she was doing something as a police officer he would totally disapprove of. She'd not spoken to him directly, calling the station early that morning to inform them she was sick, and wouldn't be attending that day. She knew Burrows wouldn't have got in that early, but that he'd be given the message as soon as he did.

He wouldn't be pleased, narrowing his bushy eyebrows and blaming the fact his rookie partner was a woman, and so couldn't be relied on.

That was just tough. In the grand scheme of things, it wasn't important.

Neither were the tears for her own precarious situation. Despite the fact that if Finn and his crew discovered her, it would be the end of everything. One more body washing ashore from a sunken old boat wouldn't raise any suspicious eyebrows, bushy or not.

Even that didn't warrant the tears. She knew she was risking her life, but that wasn't as epic as failing in her mission.

The tears were because of Daisy. Because of the look in her eyes when Daisy had told her in no uncertain terms she was their only hope. Because her friends were resigned to losing their lives, just as long as the bad guys were brought to justice.

And because her friend knew that the way things had turned out, only one person could bring about that endgame. And it wasn't going to be Daisy.

After she'd feigned throwing up, as Sarah had pressed her ear to the toilet door she'd heard the sledgehammer thumping horror into the hull; heard Finn's gloating final words as he'd passed by the closed door on his way to the deck.

And then as she'd slowly opened the door and crept to the rear well, she'd heard Daisy and Aidan's deliberately loud ninja-screams as they'd thrown themselves at the boarders to create a diversion.

It was her cue to slip onto the bathing platform. At first she'd hesitated, torn between staying by her friends' sides, and the last gasp of possibility of making justice happen. But then as she closed her eyes and willed for a sign to help her make the right decision, Daisy was there. In her mind, she was making absolutely certain Sarah knew that if she didn't take the leap of faith, everything would have been pointless.

So she'd made that leap, but it was the hardest thing she'd ever had to do. She made it because she knew for certain it was what Daisy wanted, more than anything.

She wiped away the tears, so she had clear vision to watch the old crabber dwindle to a tiny speck, and then finally disappear behind the curve of the Earth.

Suddenly, she felt alone. The enormity, and the risks of the task ahead thumped a dull ache of dread through her stomach. In essence her task was simple; just to stay on board the boat until the next evening, when it and its valuable cargo would land somewhere on the North Norfolk coastline. The Fitbit and her father's watchful eyes would do the real work, and organise a reception committee for when and where they did land.

In reality it wasn't simple at all. For the good of her health she couldn't stay on the noisy, never-still bathing platform for over twenty-four hours. It might be late summer, but already she was shivering a little, and she didn't have a sleeping bag and camping stove for the night ahead. And when Finn moored at Antwerp or wherever he was heading, someone would surely discover her.

She had to find a hiding place, which might not be too difficult in the depths of the boat. But getting there was a major problem. Surely the only way was to climb onto the rear deck? But with three crooks aboard, that was a very risky task.

She shook away the despondency, and stood slowly up. The rear transom panel of the boat was tall, made even taller as it also formed the support for the backrest of the rear deck seat. Even at her full height she could only just peep over the grab-rail at the top.

No one was on the aft deck. She could see Johnson, sitting on the rear seating of the flybridge way above her, his shaven head just visible above the backrest. Finn was almost certainly at the helm, well hidden from her view. She couldn't see any sign of Desmond, he was probably somewhere in one of the cabins.

She saw Johnson's head turn a little. He was likely just taking in the view, but she instinctively crouched back down. And then she noticed something. Her hand, pressed against the rear transom panel to give her some support, touched something that wasn't just smooth fibreglass.

The rear of the boat wasn't solid. A large, almost invisible hatch was built into it. There were two doors, but no handles, just a tiny chrome flange in each one. They were designed for vain and rich owners to appear like they weren't there at all. A key... some kind of key was needed to release the doors.

Her heart sank. There was no key. She looked around. A set of fibreglass teak-treaded steps was built-in to the superstructure, curving down from a low access door in the rear deck to the bathing platform. Where the sidewall of the steps met the transom at right-angles, there was a built-in rectangular pocket.

Her heart thumping, she felt inside.

The key.

She felt like screaming her joy, but managed to stay silent, telling herself it was probably just some kind of locker anyway.

It wasn't a locker. As she turned the key and eased open one of the doors, it was a much bigger space. A tiny garage, almost filled by two jet-skis.

Again her heart sank. It was one step better than a bathing platform open to the elements, but it was designed to fit two jet-skis, with very little room for anyone to spend time there in any kind of comfort. But then she noticed another, smaller hatch in the far wall. Which might just lead to the rest of the boat.

She squeezed into the small garage space, grateful she was as slender and supple as she was. There was a little more room between the bikes and the end wall with the hatch. But as she looked it over, she saw it wasn't exactly a big opening. She would have to be a contortionist again to get through it.

It wasn't exactly quiet either. The sound of the engines was louder, and with the additional thumping of waves on hull, her ears were buzzing in a confused kind of way. She shook her head, trying to ignore the audio torture, and used the key in her hand to unlock the hatch.

And then she realised why the engine noise was so loud. The hatch opened onto the engine room, the two big diesels sitting side by side, clattering away as Finn was forcing them to work their hardest. Then she realised something else.

Suddenly, she knew exactly where the delectable Desmond was.

Chapter 35

Daisy and Aidan, their arms around each other, watched for a couple of minutes as the sleek white luxury cruiser dwindled to a speck, the tiny forlorn figure still sitting hunched on the bathing platform like a lonely Tinkerbelle.

'Did we do the right thing, dear?' Daisy asked, wiping a tear from her eye.

He looked lovingly into her sad eyes. 'If I'm honest, Sarah stands a better chance than we do of surviving this. And a hundred percent better chance of bringing Finn down.'

'It doesn't make me feel so good though.'

There were no words to make either of them feel any better. He kissed her on the forehead. 'So what now? You said you had another phone somewhere?'

She began to fumble around underneath her outer garments. 'Yes, and you don't need to know where that somewhere is. Go and see what our planking situation is, while I check out the wheelhouse.'

'Oh, dear god...' He left her to retrieve the phone, and disappeared through the doors, heading to the bow.

As soon as he stepped through the tiny door into the chain locker, his heart sank to the rather wet floor. Water was pouring through the gap in the separated hull plank, and already he was standing in three inches of water.

He looked around for something to plug the gap, but found nothing. Quickly he stepped back out to one of the cabins, grabbed a couple of pillows and tried to stuff them into the gap. He managed it, but within seconds he could see there were damp patches appearing through them.

He groaned to himself, and was about to say 'bugger' until he realised the situation had gone way beyond that.

182

Then he heard the engine note rise, as Daisy thrust to throttle lever to full.

And straightaway he could tell that her well-meaning act wasn't well-meaning at all, as far as their health was concerned.

She was gripping the wheel like her life depended on it as he made the wheelhouse. 'Dear, you've got to stop. Moving forward is just forcing the water to pour in faster.'

She eased the throttle back, turned to him. 'That's a bugger then, Dip.'

He glanced around at the various electronic gadgetry surrounding the wheel. 'Looks like Johnson had a bit of fun before he left.'

She grimaced. 'Radio and radar monitor smashed. No chance of communicating that way. How's the North Sea below decks?'

'Coming in fast. Tried to stem the flow but no chance of anything more than very temporary delaying tactics I'm afraid. What about the phone?'

She glanced at the ancient blue Nokia in her hand. 'Apart from the fact this old thing is small enough to hide in the tiniest crevice, there's no phone signal.'

'Bugger.'

'Things aren't looking too good, dear. There is one saving grace, but it stands a slim chance of working. You know this is my phone from my previous life, right?'

He knew all too well. 'But the last time we used the satellite link was three years ago... surely the access codes have changed?'

'As I said, it has a slim chance of working.'

'I remember back then you told me the satellite link could be accessed from any mobile phone, but you had to possess the code to do so. Even if it still works, can you remember it?'

'Dear, you of little faith! It's on speed-dial!'

'Daisy! That's a secret government code,' he gasped.

'So right now, you're chastising me for that?'

He grinned, even though it was the last thing he felt like doing. 'It'll never work though.'

Rupert deWinter was enjoying his evening dinner. Close to retirement, he was winding down his hours at the central London office, and just starting to make more time to enjoy life. It was his sixtieth birthday, and the meal at the Horseguards with his wife and two of their friends was relaxing, and superbly delicious.

For someone in his position, retiring from a long career where nine-to-five didn't really exist was going to be hard. But pleasant evenings like they were having, when he could finally take a break from the stresses of his high-ranking position, really did help prepare him for the sea-changes ahead. He was looking forward to many more such evenings, and the time he could properly be there for his wife and their children.

Then his phone rang.

He almost hadn't brought it that evening, not wishing to be disturbed so close to the day when he definitely wouldn't be, but old habits die hard. He pulled it out of his jacket pocket, and frowned curiously at it. The ringtone, and the little symbol on the screen, told him the call was coming through the satellite network.

'Yes? Who is this?'

The voice was crackly, distant. 'It's Daisy.'

'Daisy? How the hell...'

'Long story. But we've got a situation here.'

His wife and their friends were looking at him in a puzzled kind of way. He apologised, excused himself, and walked into the almost-deserted foyer. 'Daisy, are you ok?'

'Um... not really. Stuck on a sinking boat on the North Sea, and no way to escape. Really could do with your assistance, Rupert.'

He took a moment to digest the unexpected caller, and the even more unexpected words. 'Daisy, you do get yourself into some scrapes.'

'Well, this one is seriously life-threatening, so are you going to help or not?'

He couldn't stop a grin at the attitude he'd not heard for three years. 'I'll get onto the coastguard right now. Give me your coordinates, please.'

'Um... no can do. Somewhere between England and Belgium the best I can say.'

'Daisy! That's an awful lot of ocean. Ok, leave your phone on. They'll try and track you from that.'

'Um... that might be an issue too. All I have on me is my old Nokia, which has been searching for signal all day. You know what that does to ancient phones. Now I'm using the satellite link, there's only three percent charge left.'

'Oh boy. Ok, hang in there. I'll do what I can, but you're the proverbial needle in the haystack.'

'It's not hayfever that's worrying me, Rupert.'

'I guess not.'

He started to say something else, but the link went dead. Daisy's phone had died. He dialled a number, and spoke to his number two, fortunately still in the office. Then he headed back into the restaurant, to tell his wife and their friends the evening was over.

Chapter 36

Sarah quietly closed the hatch door to the engine room. Desmond was facing away from her, busy carrying out some kind of maintenance-type duty.

She didn't think he'd seen her. He certainly wouldn't have heard her, given the soul-destroying noise in the confines of the engine room. She sank to her knees, all she had room to do in the jet-ski bay, and waited for the sounds of the hatch opening that would tell her she was wrong.

Nothing happened. He hadn't seen her. She resigned herself to waiting it out before she tried again, consoling herself that given the noise and the stifling conditions in the engine room, he wouldn't be there any longer than he had to be.

Twenty minutes later she struggled to her feet again, slipped the key into the hole and turned it slowly. Luckily it was hinged at the bottom, not designed for humans to use it as a designated route. She didn't have to let it open too far to see she wasn't wrong, and the engine room was devoid of life.

It was time to make a move. She folded her body almost double, suckered herself through the tiny hatch, and almost fell onto the engine room floor. Quickly she straightened herself up, panning her eyes around the much bigger space to make sure she was indeed alone.

The low-powered lights were on, and she could see easily enough no one was there. Feeling like the stowaway she actually was, she crept closer to the aluminium ladder leading to the main deck of the boat. The access hatch above her was shut, and it looked like Desmond had finished whatever he was doing.

Her head was three inches from the low ceiling, and she smiled to herself at the lack of vertical stature her five foot four possessed. She'd always cursed the fact a large swathe of the population seemed to tower over her for most of her life, but right then she was so grateful for it, and the room she finally had to stretch her stiff body back to life.

The ridiculously-tall Desmond must have had to stoop like hell to get around.

A narrow doorway was set into the forward bulkhead. She crept over to it, and pulled it open. It was the chain locker, with storage shelves either side of the door, containing marine-type bits and bobs. They ended in a pair of half-bulkheads, and then the space opened out to the full width of the bow, partly filled by two piles of chains. Each chain disappeared through a hole set high up in the hull, where their final links were undoubtedly the anchors that sat against the bow, waiting patiently for the time they were needed.

The triangular space brought a smile to Sarah's face. She closed the door, knowing she'd discovered her penthouse for the rest of the trip. The boat's kind designers had found the space for a small bench, and fitted a tiny porthole on each side of the hull. The last light of the day was shining through, and giving the rather stark space, it was to her a beautiful, mellow glow.

The hard wooden bench top wasn't big enough to stretch out on, but in the foetal position she might just about manage a few hours sleep. And the view through the two portholes would tell her where she was, and give her a clue what was going on around her.

Feeling like she'd won the lottery and just bought herself a Mayfair apartment, she sank onto the firmness of the bench, and let out a sigh of relief.

She'd have to keep an eye and an ear out for anyone coming, and if they did there was literally nowhere to escape... but the likelihood of someone finding her there was remote. The tiny room served a purpose that didn't need much human intervention.

She allowed herself to close her eyes. The heat from the engines permeated through into the penthouse, and made it a little stifling. She'd opened the portholes, just a little in case someone noticed, but it hadn't helped much. Finally, she could rest in relative peace. She pulled off her jumper and balled it up, laid it onto the pile of chain next to the bench to make a crude pillow, and settled back to enjoy the journey.

Something jolted her back to consciousness. For a second she felt angry with herself. She'd tried so hard not to fall asleep, but the relaxation from the joy of finding herself a bolt-hole had decided otherwise.

It was dark. She glanced at the Fitbit, and shocked herself as she realised she'd been asleep for four hours. She sat up, her body telling her the hard unforgiving bench had forced it to discover bones it never knew it had.

She glanced through the tiny porthole. She could see land, about a mile away in the gloom. As she watched for a moment, a small container ship passed by, heading the other way. She stood up, a little painfully, and peered through the porthole on the starboard side of the bow. There was land there too, a little closer.

They were in some kind of wide estuary. She closed her eyes, thought back to her schooldays, and the geography lessons she disliked so much. But the recall helped her to remember that Antwerp wasn't right on the North Sea coast. It was several miles inland, reached by ships through a wide estuary, rather like London.

She sucked in a deep, faltering breath. The first leg of her journey was almost over, and she realised what had woken her. The engine note had changed, Finn reducing the speed a little as they grew close to land. The motion of the boat had lessened too, the low hills on either side sheltering the water from the winds of the North Sea.

Was he going to cruise right into Antwerp port? She couldn't know, not right then. There were plenty of bays and landing stages for the rest of the journey, a myriad of tiny fishing villages that had grown up over time in the sheltered waters.

It wasn't long until she knew. As she watched through the porthole the boat turned to the right, and a minute later, a long wooden landing stage loomed out of the darkness. A half-mile further up the hill, the lights of a very European chateau-style residence blazed out across formal lawns that sloped down to the water.

It all looked very opulent, and very baroque. And it was clearly their final destination.

She watched as two men on the stage grabbed the ropes the crew threw to them, and wrapped them around wooden bollards on the landing stage, brightly lit by low-level lamps. Then the two men made their way back to the house, and were gone from her sight.

Two minutes later there was silence. Finn killed the engines, and all Sarah could hear was the sound of gentle waves lapping against the hull. Then came the muffled thump of three pairs of feet dropping onto the landing stage, and a moment later, the men she knew too well

189

passed by, heading in the direction of the house, completely unaware a stowaway was still hiding on the boat.

Just as they passed by, through the open porthole she heard Finn's delighted voice, as he wrapped an arm around the shoulders of each of his colleagues.

'Well gentlemen, a successful day, was it not? Now let us enjoy the delights created by my mother's cook, and a good night's sleep in her sumptuous bedrooms. But don't be getting too inebriated, the delivery man will be here at the crack of dawn, and we'll be on our merry way back again.'

He laughed the relaxed laugh of a man who thought he'd solved all his problems, and the two other men laughed in agreement. Then they were gone, and Sarah had her little world to herself.

She pressed her lips determinedly together at his lordship's words, which speared a dagger of pain into her young heart.

'Enjoy your victory while you can, Finn,' she muttered under her breath.

Chapter 37

'It's big, isn't it?'

Aidan knew straightaway what Daisy meant. He slipped an arm around her as they stood on the deck, watching the sun disappear below the watery horizon.

'It's huge. But they'll find us, before...'

'Before we get wet?' She rested her head on his shoulder. 'It's a massive search area, dear. We've no idea where we are, and the phone is dead now. It's visual location only, and we're but a tiny speck.'

'Maybe it's time for you to have faith, Flower. Like you tell me to do, quite often.'

She pulled him tight to her. 'How long do you think we have before our ship goes down, dear?'

'I don't know. An hour, maybe two. Just don't call me Jack, Rose.'

She found a smile. 'This time, Mr. Dawson, we will both live to fight another day.'

He cast fearful eyes to the bow of the old crabber. It had only been ten minutes since the call to Rupert had miraculously managed to get through to him, and already he could tell the front of the boat was a little lower in the water than it had been when they first boarded.

It was a beautiful nautical sunset, the virtually cloudless sky turning an enticing shade of salmon, which darkened relentlessly to crimson as the light faded. But the lack of land in any direction sent a dull ache of dread through his stomach. Well away from either coast, Daisy's comment was an extremely relevant one. It was big. And it was empty.

As the day said goodbye, the swell had faded along with the light. The North Sea was like a millpond, just the faintest of undulations rippling the surface.

There were no icebergs in sight, but Daisy's comparison stabbed a horrific dagger into his soul.

It was almost dark. A full moon had climbed a little way into the sky, a beacon of faint hope that would at least help the searchers to find them, and give them a ghostly light to watch their own demise.

A short while ago they'd spotted two commercial ships, but they were both a long way off, and neither stood a chance of seeing their tiny craft. Captain Hook knew what he was doing, making sure that when they were scuppered it was well away from the regular shipping lanes.

They sat huddled together on the roof of the cabin, watching as the stars seemed to appear from nowhere, slowly studding the sky that only had the faintest tinge of dark blue left, just above the western horizon. The lights from the wheelhouse cast a welcoming glow across the deck in front of them, but they both knew once the water reached the batteries, those lights would be no more.

There hadn't been a lot of conversation in the hour they'd been sitting there. Daisy had remarked in typical Daisy-fashion that her butt seemed to be closer to the sea, and Aidan had replied that he was grateful his butt and hers were the only two butts sinking lower.

One hour and five minutes after they'd sat on the cabin roof, the wheelhouse lights crackled and died. For a moment all seemed dark, and then their eyes tuned into the moonlight reflecting off the almost-millpond around them, and then it didn't seem so dark.

'It's kind of beautiful, you know,' said Daisy quietly, slipping her hand into Aidan's.

'It is. I never realised how beautiful it was, sitting on the roof of a sinking boat, being able to see the ocean like I've never seen it before.'

She glanced curiously to him, detecting no sarcasm in his tone. Then she realised there was no sarcasm. He meant every word.

'I'm glad it's just you and me. If we're facing endgame, this is as good a way as any.'

She saw his head lower. 'Thank you, darling,' he whispered.

'They're not going to find us, are they? Not until...until it's too late.'

'We're not wet yet, dear.'

The conversation died for a couple of minutes. They weren't wet yet, but the time for a salty soaking wasn't far away. Even on the roof of the cabin, the surface of the ocean didn't seem that far below them. The time was fast approaching when the old crabber would gasp her last breath, and be gone forever.

'You know what I regret most of all?'

'Of course I do. I regret it too,' Aidan said, resting his head against Daisy's.

She waved an arm at the dark horizon, and then lifted it to aim at the stars. 'Do you think Celia is out there somewhere... or up there?'

'I wish more than anything I could tell you, but if I said anything now, you'd know it wasn't based on fact.'

'Tell me anyway?'

'In my heart, I think she's out there somewhere... not up there...' he pointed to the heavens.

She turned her head, and kissed him softly. 'Thank you. I believe that too.' Her head dropped to the deck, and the moonlight reflected off the gloss of tears in her eyes. 'But now we'll never know for sure, will we?'

He put both arms around her, and pulled them as tight as he could. Answering the question that wasn't a question at all just wasn't necessary. And he didn't want her to hear the defeated tone that would have cracked his voice.

Ten minutes later the silent peace was shattered. The old boat seemed to shudder beneath them. Ripped from her tranquil thoughts, Daisy glanced up, and peered ahead. She couldn't see the bow. 'Dear, there's only minutes left. We have to do something to avoid drowning for as long as possible.'

He cast his eyes around. Just behind them, a large hatch formed part of the cabin roof. Like the rest of the boat, it was made of wood. He turned round, felt around it. 'It seems to be hinged, not fixed.'

'Yes, I saw the stays inside the walkway roof.'

'Help me. Maybe we can wrench it free.'

They tried, but held firm by the internal stays, it wouldn't budge. 'I'll have to release the stays from inside first,' Aidan said, heading for the rear well and the access doors.

'Dear, it's going to be half under water. Be careful...'

He was gone. Forcing open the rear doors, he groaned. 'Bugger.' Two feet of water covered the floor. Daisy was right, there was only minutes left. He splashed his way to the hatch, and glanced up. The stays were relatively new, part of the conversion. They didn't look that substantial. He reached up, grabbed hold of them and used his bodyweight to rip them away from their fixings.

He splashed his way back to Daisy. 'Now... lift!'

Grabbing one side each, the hatch lifted up. But it was still hinged on one side. 'Push it right back... let it fall hard!'

They raised the hatch to just past its vertical point, and let go. Not designed for such a crazy angle, as it fell back the hinges ripped away from their screws, and the hatch crashed down to the deck.

'Onto the safety rail...'

They manhandled the six-foot hatch so it was balancing on the iron rail. 'Now shove it over, and then jump. And then swim like hell, because when this old lady goes down we might get caught in the vortex...'

The hatch tipped over into the dark water. It didn't have far to fall, the ocean just a couple of feet below the deck. Daisy jumped after it, and for a moment her world was nothing but seawater. Then she bobbed up to the surface. The hatch was right next to her; she grabbed its edge and began to kick crazily with her feet. For a second she couldn't see Aidan, and a stab of panic flooded her heart.

'Aidan!'

Then he was there, his silver hair plastered to his forehead as he gasped in a lungful of air. Together they kicked themselves away from the boat. They'd made twenty feet when the old girl seemed to wheeze a deathly cry, and disappeared below the surface.

The water around them began to swirl. Daisy grasped the hatch as tightly as she could, and as the merry-go-round turned their world to a mess of spinning movement she closed her eyes, and began to wonder if a slightly-premature endgame had happened after all.

Then Aidan's watery shout made her open her eyes again, and she realised their lonely world was calm once more.

'Climb on the hatch. It should hold your weight.'

'Seriously? My name isn't really Rose, you know.'

'Will you just do as I say for once?'

She did as he said, and managed to drag her soggy body onto the hatch. She held out a hand to help him up, still treading water with his arms across the top of the hatch. He spluttered out the words.

'No dear... it'll never support both our weights.'

'Oh, come on. Really?'

'It's ok... it's a warm August sea, not an iceberg-strewn April one. I can hold on for a while.'

'I don't believe this... so can I call you Jack now?'

He laughed. 'My name is Aidan... and it will be for a few years yet... hopefully.'

She put her hands around his soaking cheeks. 'What would I do without you, hey?'

'Just kiss me, while I've got the strength to kiss you back.'

She kissed him, and then grasped his arms and held onto them for dear life. She didn't let him see her heart was breaking, just smiled encouragement to him instead. She knew as well as he that survival hung by a more fragile thread than it had ever done before.

They'd escaped the sinking of the crabber by the skin of their teeth. But their new precarious situation could never last for long. In Daisy's mind they were cheating time, when ultimately it would refuse to be cheated. There were no more words to say. All she could do was never let go of him, and pray.

But miracles do happen twice.

Suddenly their watery world was a mass of bright light. And an angel came to visit, suspended in the air, right above them.

An angel dressed in an RAF flying suit, dangling from a rope, with a rescue cradle in his arms.

Chapter 38

Sarah gave it a couple of hours. It was almost midnight, and her empty stomach was reminding her of that. She'd had no food, but she knew where she would likely find some.

A short while ago her eyes had misted up as her thoughts inevitably turned to Daisy and Aidan. Their chances of survival were pretty slim, but she had no way of knowing if that slim chance had proved to be a good one. She wouldn't know any different for another day, but right then she had a job to do... a job that might prove to be a reason their sacrifice was as worthwhile as it could possibly be.

She had to make sure she remained a secret stowaway until Finn and his cargo got back to Norfolk. If she was discovered, everything would have been a tragic waste. But she couldn't do it on an empty stomach.

Her world was in darkness. The lights on the landing stage had been switched off a while ago, and it was a pretty safe bet Finn and his crew were tucked up in their sumptuous beds in the chateau, along with everyone else. Watching through the tiny porthole, apart from the commercial vessels which passed by every few minutes, not a sign of life broke the tranquillity.

She had to make a move, to ensure she seized her opportunity while she was alone. Collapsing from hunger before she was able to instigate the final stage of the plan wouldn't get the job done. She eased open the narrow door to the engine room. That was in darkness too, a black hole that felt spooky, and more than a little scary.

She had to feel her way to the ladder, but as she climbed the few steps and eased open the hatch to the upper floor of the boat, a little light flooded in. It was a full moon, which cast equally-spooky shadows around the stateroom, but was one step better than complete blackness.

She tiptoed across the carpet. Even in the moonlight, the opulence of the luxury cruiser was obvious. Plush seating ran along two sides, one side curving into a half-height division to separate it from the part of the boat she needed.

She shook her head. The galley was bigger than the one in her annex at home, and far better equipped. A combined oven and microwave sat in a tall unit next to a curving run of cupboards topped by a fine-quality granite worktop with a gas hob set into it. Next to the tall housing was another one, with three doors, the larger of which was set in the centre.

It was very likely the fridge, sitting behind an integrated door to hide its ugliness from the rich owner. She reached out to the handle, and pulled it open a little. A shaft of light flooded out across the floor. Instantly she closed it again, and glanced furtively around.

She was right, it was the fridge. But fridges have internal lights, the last thing she needed to illuminate a supposedly-unoccupied boat if someone was watching and happened to spot it. She looked up to the old house. Just one light shone from an upstairs window, but the curtains were closed. No one seemed to be around, but then again, no one had any reason to suspect all was not as well as they assumed it was.

She had to risk it, her stomach was persuading her of that. Just from a quick glance she'd seen the full-sized fridge was stacked with food. A few bits going missing would never be noticed, but even if it was, Finn would likely assume one of his crew had simply got a bit hungry.

She had to be quick. She opened the door as little as possible, rapidly scanned the contents, reached in and grabbed a few morsels of food, and a can of Irish beer. In the back of one of the drawers she found a carrier bag, stuffed her stolen stash into it, and then watched for ten minutes to make sure no one had noticed the light that shouldn't exist.

All was quiet. She sank onto the deep padded seating, and ate a little of the food. She'd have to ration it; a second trip to the fridge would be out of the question.

It was so tempting to curl up on the opulent sofa and grab a few hours sleep, but she resisted the urge. There was no telling when the crew would return to prepare the ship for its homeward cruise, and if she was discovered like Snow White, the game would be up for sure.

So reluctantly she headed back to the dark confines of her penthouse. As she sank onto the hard bench, she breathed a sigh of relief. She'd got a small stash of food to see her through the day ahead, and as long as no one came to the chain locker, her plan stood a fair chance of working.

She smiled a half-satisfied but nervous smile to herself, settled back, and cracked open the can of beer.

– – –

Daisy, her head shrouded by a thick silver thermal blanket, and her hand firmly wrapped around the similarly-shrouded Aidan's, smiled to the young female RAF air-sea-rescue sergeant sitting opposite her.

'Where are you taking us, dear?' she shouted through the noise of the engine.

'The Norfolk and Norwich hospital. You need to be checked out.'

'Oh no, dear. That's not acceptable. We're fine.' She glanced to Aidan, 'You are fine, aren't you, darling?'

'What?'

'I said, you're fine, aren't you?'

'If you say so, dear.'

'Yes, we're fine. Take us to Wells-on-Sea, please.' She looked at Aidan again. 'You have still got the car keys, I assume?

'What?'

'I said, you have still got the car keys?'

He fumbled in the very soggy inside pocket of his jacket, and nodded.

'Wells-on-Sea then, please.'

The guy sitting next to his sergeant, who had been their angel on the end of a rope, looked a little perturbed. 'Our orders are to make sure you get checked out, ma'am.'

Daisy shook her head. 'Dear boy, thank you for rescuing us, but we have to recover our car. It's a matter of life and death.'

He looked puzzled. 'But we've just rescued you.'

'Not ours... look, just take us to Wells, please.'

The sergeant was shaking her head. 'After you've been checked out, someone will...'

'Do you know who I am, sergeant?'

'Well, no. But I was told the order to search for you came from a... high level.'

'Well, there you go then. I'll just say it is better you don't know who I am. But I'm countermanding your order, sergeant.'

'But you... you're...'

201

'Old? So everyone keeps telling me. Don't let appearances fool you. Now, are you taking us to Wells or not?

It was three in the morning when the yellow helicopter touched down onto the almost empty car park opposite the harbour in Wells. And as it lifted off again, a few faces at windows watched curiously as it appeared that two senior citizens had clambered out alone. It was nothing unusual for the residents of Wells to see the yellow helicopters flying low over the town.

It was very unusual to see one land in the harbour car park, in the early hours of the morning.

Daisy waved cheerily to the pilot and his crew as the chopper flew off into the darkness. Then she grabbed Aidan's arm, and dragged him quickly to the BMW, standing just a few yards away.

'Get me home, dear. I need a brandy or five.'

He glanced to her as the car drove down the narrow main street, 'You'll be the death of me, Flower.'

She found a grin from somewhere. 'I very nearly was, Dip. But sometimes my old employment comes in handy. Like when it saves both our lives, and when I need to make out to the air-sea-rescue crew it's my current employment!'

Chapter 39

Daisy virtually fell through the side door into the kitchen, and made a beeline for the brandy bottle.

'Don't tell me to go steady, Dip.'

He followed her in. 'Wasn't going to. But we both need to get out of these clothes.'

She thrust a glass in his hand. 'Brandy first. Then dry clothes.'

He nodded his agreement, noticing the shudder racking her body. 'Was that the damp, or the emotions kicking in?'

She downed the brandy, gave him a grin. 'Both. Plus the pure joy of the alcohol going down. Ok, dry clothes, and then we make a phone call.'

Warm and cosy in her hooded dressing gown, Daisy flicked through the online phone book, 'There's only one Lowry listed in East Winch, dear. It has to be him.'

Standing next to her, he wrapped a hand around her shoulder. 'It's four in the morning, Daisy. He might not appreciate a phone call at this hour.'

'Dear, if he's anything like you and me, he won't be getting any sleep this night.'

She picked up the landline phone, and dialled the number. Five seconds later, a nervous voice answered. 'Yes? David Lowry here.'

'Mr. Lowry, it's Daisy Morrow...'

'Daisy? Where are you? Is my daughter with you?'

His voice gave away the panic the sudden phone call had brought him. 'Um... no. We got... separated. She's a stowaway on Finn's boat...'

'Oh my god... I knew this was a bad idea...'

'Mr. Lowry...' She brought him up to speed with a nutshell version of recent events. He didn't seem too pleased with what he heard.

'So by now anything could have happened, and we have no way of knowing? We need to get the Belgian authorities involved.'

Daisy glanced up to Aidan. Sarah's father was right, but he was also wrong. Aidan grabbed the phone, as Daisy buried her face in her hands. 'Mr. Lowry, it's Aidan Henderson. Look, it's probably too late for that. In the next couple of hours they'll be heading back to England. I know it's hard for you... god knows it's hard enough for us, but Sarah is determined to see this through to its conclusion, and I think we must have faith in her, and do the same.'

There was silence for a few seconds. When he spoke again, his voice was choked with fear. 'I suppose you're right. I'd never hear the end of it if we alerted Poirot now. It's just not knowing...'

Aidan nodded his head. 'You don't need to tell us about that. But we should be in the same place. Do we come to you or do you want to come to us?'

'You two have just been through hell. Stay in the warm, get a couple of hours sleep. I'll come to you at nine, if that's ok?'

Aidan said it was, gave him the address, and put down the phone. Then he wrapped his arms around Daisy. 'You heard the man. Let's go shuggle up for a while. Tonight is going to be a big night.'

Daisy's eyes looked over Sarah's father as she handed him a cup of coffee. In his fifties, he was roughly the same age as Burrows, but where the inspector had carried on plodding, David Lowry had taken early retirement.

She'd noticed the slight limp as he'd walked through the door two minutes ago. Whether it was a health-related limp, or one incurred by an altercation with the wrong criminal, she didn't know. But it was very likely the desk-based position they'd offered him wasn't something he'd wanted to accept.

His sandy hair was cropped short, and almost certainly the colour that would never go grey. His eyes weren't the sunken, dead eyes of Burrows. There was still a light behind them, and the same determined look Daisy had recognised in his daughter's. He'd clearly got out before it all became too much a part of him.

The strained, desperate lines on his face weren't the result of years of stress. More the result of hours of stress. It was pretty obvious they'd clashed when Sarah told him of her plan B a day ago. He'd most likely said she'd lost her mind, in a very vociferous way, and told her not to do it. But Daisy already knew Sarah possessed the same stubbornness she did, and he would have known that no matter how much he protested, he was on a losing wicket.

Aidan shook his hand. 'None of us like this, Mr. Lowry. There's no way we can contact Sarah, no way to know...'

He shook his head, 'Please, call me David. This waiting is driving me crazy, and now you've told me what you have, the uncertainty is even harder to handle.'

Daisy put a hand on his arm. 'We feel the same, David. But your daughter is resourceful and determined. I know she's fine, and on her way back to us right now.'

She wished she could have sounded more convinced, and as David nodded slowly and silently, that didn't look very convincing either. She tried to be a little more practical, take all their minds off what might or might not have happened. 'Ok... it's going to be this evening until we know anything from Sarah's Fitbit, but before then we've got to make plans for the final showdown. I take it you know Burrows, David?'

'We used to work together, yes.'

'So telling him what's going down, and persuading him to mobilise his forces will be better coming from you, rather than a pair of nosy, geriatric busybodies, I assume?'

'Oh, for sure. We did rather clash now and again, but from one copper to another, you know?'

'Trust me, I know. And I'm afraid Aidan and me did rather... emphasise our senior citizen-ness, so he doesn't have a very high opinion of us. Much better coming from you!'

'So what do you want me to do?'

'Finish your coffee while we strategise, and then I think you should go and sit down face-to-face with your ex-colleague, and make sure he gets his ass into gear.'

Chapter 40

The time drifted past seven in the evening, and still there was no sign of nautical life from the Fitbit. Outside, the shadows creeping over the village of Great Wiltingham grew longer, the sun slipping close to the horizon as the day of waiting prepared to come to an end.

Inside, things weren't so tranquil. Aidan had rigged Sarah's phone to the PC, so the three of them could see the map of North Norfolk without peering at a tiny screen. But big or small, there was still nothing there to see.

Finn's reception committee was ready and waiting. Burrows had initially thrown a few things around in anger when David went to see him, spouting about violations of police procedure and stubborn female officers disobeying orders, but once he'd calmed down, even he could see the potential danger.

And the potential pats on the back his department would get if everything went to plan.

So he got on the phone, organised his own people and the drugs squad, who then demanded access to Sarah's phone, and the app that would tell them where the suspect was landing.

David refused, ignoring Burrows' glare, and telling them that as soon as he knew where the drop point was, they would too.

He'd kept Daisy and Aidan's name out of it, at their request, not quite telling the whole truth. Interfering old codgers were the last thing Burrows needed, even if they were the ones who had made much of it happen. As far as the inspector knew right then, Sarah had stowed away on a hunch, based on certain information she had discovered.

Daisy had smiled to herself when David told her he'd said nothing about them. She knew herself all too well, and she knew Burrows would get the whole truth shoved in front of him before too long anyway.

None of that made any of them feel better right then. The day was coming to an end, and while they all knew Finn would only land after dark, the one thing they didn't know was if Sarah had been discovered. There was something else they weren't sure of either.

'What's the range of that Fitbit GPS app, David?'

He shook a desolate head. 'No idea. Only twenty of thirty miles maybe, but she should have been in range by now.'

Aidan tried to reassure him. 'Not necessarily. We don't know what speed Finn was cruising at. It might be midnight before he actually lands.'

An equally-desolate Daisy glared at him. 'Did you have to say that?'

'Just trying to help, dear.'

'Well don't.'

It wasn't midnight. An hour, and three shots of brandy later, the screen pinged.

A faint red dot appeared. Then, infuriatingly, it disappeared again. They looked at each other, probably to make sure none of them had imagined it.

'Do you think..?'

Five seconds later the beautiful ping filled their ears again. The red dot was back, glowing stronger as three pairs of eyes stared at it in a slightly-disbelieving way.

'Oh my god...'

David was on his feet, pulling Daisy into a tight hug, and then looking embarrassed as he eased away and wiped the tears from his eyes. 'Sorry. It's her, isn't it?'

Daisy pulled him back tight to her. 'Don't be sorry, you silly man. It has to be her... doesn't it?' she glanced to Aidan, aiming the question at him.

'Well unless someone out in the North Sea has hacked her app, then it surely is.' He turned away, wiping the moisture from his eyes.

Somehow, Daisy pulled herself together, and turned back to the monitor. 'Ok... relieved and joyful emotions aside, this isn't over yet. Look, they're still out at sea.'

Aidan peered at the screen. 'Hmm, according to this, they're a good ten miles off shore. But Finn still seems to be heading for Wells.'

David narrowed his eyes. 'Surely he's not going to offload there? It's a bit public.'

'I doubt it,' said Daisy. But there's a lot of far less public coastline close by. I doubt he'll deviate far from the expected route.'

'I'll call Burrows, tell him it's game on.'

They watched the screen, hardly blinking as the red dot slowly headed closer to the shoreline. Still it looked like the boat was making for Wells. Still Daisy wasn't prepared to accept that was where he was going.

But then, two miles offshore, the dot took a left turn. Aidan zoomed in a little, and glanced to the others. It was almost ten in the evening, totally dark, and it looked like Finn was preparing for the final stage of his journey home.

Still the red dot was heading south, and as he scrolled down the map a little further, they could see there was only one place he could be heading.

'He's aiming for the River Glaven,' Aidan said quietly.

Daisy shook her head. 'Blakeney. Or maybe Morston Quay. We went there in May. But there's a public car park, and a visitor centre and ice-cream kiosk. It's popular with boaters and coast-walkers. It's still a bit public to be ideal, I would have thought.'

'Not after dark. When night falls it's pretty desolate, and well away from the village itself.'

'But easy access for anyone who wants to meet a random boat without anyone seeing.'

Daisy headed for the office door. 'Ok guys, time to get there, now. David, keep your eyes on that phone screen. And tell Burrows it's somewhere close to Morston Quay!'

He got to his feet. 'He won't be too pleased to see you two there.'

'Tough. You think we're going to miss seeing Finn get his comeuppance? And quite frankly, I can't wait to see his face when he sets eyes on us!'

Chapter 41

Five minutes before they reached the village of Morston, David called out from the back seat. 'They've just turned down Morston Creek. Looks like we were right, there doesn't seem to be anywhere else to go now except Morston Quay. I'll tell Burrows.'

'We're almost there. Drive slower, Dip. And I can't believe I'm saying that.'

David closed the call. 'Burrows says they're waiting in the village. Proceeding to the quay now.'

Daisy narrowed her eyes. 'It's quite a big area, from what I remember. Little landing stages everywhere. Keep your eye on that screen, David.'

Aidan drove down the quiet main street, and turned left into the little lane to the quay, just before the sharp bend in the road. They drove slowly into the deserted public car park. Daisy let out a little shiver. The dark hulks of a few boats on the hard-standing seemed to be surrounding them, and the moon chose that moment to go behind a cloud, making the whole scene just that little bit spookier.

'I can't see any vans or anything,' she whispered, even though no one else could possibly have heard her outside the car.

'Why are you whispering?' said Aidan.

'I don't know. It just seemed appropriate,' she whispered back.

'We need to drive up to where the landing stages are.'

Daisy looked back to David. 'Where are they now?'

'Just north of the first landing stages. Still moving.'

'Ok, park here, Dip. It might be wise to walk. If Finn's up on that flybridge thing he might see headlights.'

He pulled the BMW to a stop next to the rotting old hulk of an old cabin cruiser. As she climbed out, Daisy let out another shudder. There was hardly any wind and it wasn't cold, but it sure felt like it to her.

Aidan wrapped a reassuring arm around her. 'So where are the boys in blue?' he said as they headed for the wide gravelled road that led to the landing stages. Then, as soon as he said that, he saw two dark-coloured vans tucked up against the side of a big old fishing boat sitting on the hard.

'Well, that might be their transport,' said Daisy.

Still they could see no one. There didn't seem to be any life at all as they slipped from one dark hulk to the next, working their way to the first of the old landing stages. David was peering ahead through the gloom. A couple of hundred yards in front, the creek turned to the left. There seemed to be yet more landing stages following the bend in the creek.

But a little beyond that he could see a faint light. A powerful beam in the distance, which seemed to be moving slowly. 'Look,' he said quietly.

'That's them,' said Daisy, her voice ending in a choke. 'That's the searchlight fixed on the flybridge thing.'

Aidan grinned. 'See, I told you it'd look like the blitz!'

She thumped him, but not very hard. 'So where are the police?'

'Dunno. Let's get a little closer to the water.'

They slipped from the shelter of one dry-docked boat to the next. Then, just as they made the dark shadow of the last but one fishing boat, they froze. First it was the ratchet of an automatic rifle filling their ears. Then it was the sight of two helmeted figures pointing their guns at them.

'Stop. You're under arrest.'

Six hands flew into the air. Then a third figure came into view.

'For the love of god. You two? Again?'

Daisy threw him a big beaming smile. 'Good evening, chief inspector. Nice night for a stroll on the coast?'

'Seriously? And you, David?'

He waved the phone in the air. 'I am the one with the GPS app. And it is my daughter in danger. Did you really expect me not to be here?'

Burrows threw his hands in the air, in a half-defeated kind of way. 'Ok, fair enough. But these two have to leave. Right now.'

'Excuse me?' said Daisy indignantly.

The two officers with the guns came closer, about to obey their boss's instructions, but David stepped between them. 'Hard though it might be for you to accept, Vic, these two old cronies have played a major part in this. They might be civilians, but they have earned the right to be here. I'll make sure they don't... um, interfere.'

Burrows' mouth dropped open. 'You have got to be kidding me.' He caught the determined stare in his ex-colleague's eyes. 'You're not kidding, are you? How?'

Daisy, her eyes flicking to the spotlight getting ever nearer, put an urgent hand on Burrow's arm. 'Inspector, the fine print is for another day. Don't you think it's time to do your job?'

For a moment he couldn't find any words to reply. And in the awkward silence, they could hear the sound of the boat's engines. He silently admitted to himself there was no time for explanations. 'Back behind this boat. And don't go any further.'

213

He crept away to the cover of the last boat, but couldn't help muttering to himself as he left, 'I knew I was right about those two...'

Daisy and the others slipped back into the shadows of the old fishing boat. And five seconds later, Finn's sleek cruiser came into view around the bend. She sucked in a deep breath, reached out a hand in the darkness, and found Aidan's.

'Showtime,' she whispered.

Two hundred yards away, the boat, just about moving, headed for a rickety old landing stage. Further away, from the shelter of the lines of boats on the far end of the quay, a dark figure appeared. He didn't look like a police officer. He did know exactly where to go, walking right towards one of the landing stages before the boat had got there.

'He's a bad guy too,' Daisy whispered.

'You don't say.'

She thumped him again. 'Be quiet, dear.'

She didn't see his glare, her eyes fixed on the man, who caught the ropes Johnson and Desmond threw to him. They were tied securely to the sea-weathered bollards, and then Finn, still on the flybridge, called down.

'Greetings, my friend. It is good to be back, on this beautiful evening.'

He didn't get the chance to say anything else. Out of the shadows of the boats standing on the concourse, a platoon of dark figures brandishing guns advanced on the boat. Their cries filled the air, the silence of the tranquil night suddenly shattered, as people he sure hadn't expected to see seemed to be everywhere.

The guy who had been waiting for his delivery started to run. It only lasted a second, before he realised there was nowhere to run to. His hands shot into the air.

But Finn, who had taken a step back in horror, soon composed himself. His Irish brogue drifted down to the officers, who were now surrounding the boat, awaiting instructions from their leader.

'Gentlemen, what foolishness is this? Why, we were on our way to Wells but developed a little engine trouble, so had to land here instead. Would you not be believing a highly-respected lord of the realm?'

Burrows stepped forward from the ring of armed officers. 'Well, Lord Finnegan, would you not be believing it's a mighty coincidence that we just happened to be waiting for you at the exact place you made your emergency stop?'

''Tis a wondrous thing, is it not?'

Burrows didn't seem impressed. 'Board the boat,' he barked out to his men.

Seven or eight officers clambered aboard. In seconds, Johnson and Desmond were handcuffed, and stripped of their weapons. A still-smiling Finn was instructed to climb down to the aft deck, where he came face-to-face with Burrows.

'So, your Lordship. Good trip?'

'Well, it was until you showed up, Inspector.'

He was still smiling, and Burrows felt a little unnerved by the fact he was. The man should be devastated his life was all but over. His men were searching the boat, and any moment the real purpose of his trip to Belgium would be revealed. But still he seemed to have a smile on his face.

Two minutes later, Burrows discovered why. One of the officers ran up to him, a slightly-frustrated look on his face.

'Sir, I'm really sorry sir, but there don't seem to be any drugs on board.'

Chapter 42

Daisy, flanked by Aidan and David, had kind of ignored Burrows' instructions not to get any closer. They were still hidden in the shadows of the boats on the hard, but they'd slunk closer to the action. Finn's boat was less than fifty yards away, and the voices were carrying in the cool night air.

'No drugs?' she gasped.

'That's not possible,' said Aidan, and then shook his head. 'Bugger.'

'No, it isn't possible. The morons aren't looking hard enough.'

She marched over to the boat, and then marched right onto the aft deck, followed by Aidan and David. Then she marched right up to Finn, who was facing away from her, and switched on a smile. 'Hello, your lordship.'

He spun round, gasped, and turned a whiter shade of pale. 'You... how?'

'How what, Finn?'

He looked like he didn't know where to put himself. 'Um... how good it is to see you... Rose,' he stammered, his aristocratic cool suddenly blown away by the sea breeze.

'Oh dear boy, I'm so happy to see you too... even if I am the ghost of murders past, if you get my drift?'

For a moment he looked scared to death, no doubt suddenly getting visions of the folklore of his Irish upbringing, and seeing green leprechauns that refused to die in front of his eyes. 'I... but...'

Daisy shook her head disparagingly, and strode over to a man on the far side of the deck, who looked vaguely

217

authoritative. 'Are you the leader of the drugs squad?' she barked at him.

'Um... yes, I am.'

'Didn't you bring the dogs?'

'Well, no... it's just a small boat. We didn't want them barking at the wrong moment.'

'Useless.' Daisy turned on her pink wellie heels, and stomped into the opulent stateroom, followed by Aidan and David. She glanced around the acres of plush seating, the fabric-lined roof, and then threw a momentary glance across the galley area.

Then she turned, and peered at the main bulkhead which separated the room from the aft deck. One wall to the side of the entrance doors was adorned with a large, original oil painting, which obviously wasn't bought from a charity shop. She lifted it off its hook, and inspected the walnut woodgrained wall behind it.

It was solid, no hidden hatch panels. She growled, threw the expensive painting to the floor, and then grunted her satisfaction as she saw the glass smash, and a couple of slight tears appear in the canvas.

The good lord, standing in the doorway, looked aghast. 'Do you have any idea what that cost?'

'Oh do be quiet,' she said, turning her gaze to the left side of the doors. Fastened to the wall was a huge fifty-five inch flat-screen TV. She frowned slightly, noticing the panel holding the TV was slightly further into the stateroom than the other side. It was only a few inches, and designed to conceal wires, cables and speakers. But it fired up Daisy's curiosity.

'Dear, would you and David remove that TV please?' she said to Aidan.

The two men clambered onto the plush seating, each grabbing one side of the screen. A small crowd seemed to be gathering in the stateroom to watch the action, including his lordship, who wasn't looking as pleased with life as he was half an hour ago.

The TV lifted away from the bulkhead. It was quite heavy, and Aidan called out, 'What about the wires, Daisy? We don't have a free hand to disconnect them...'

'Just rip them out,' Daisy grinned.

'Oh, I say...' said Finn.

'If you say so, dear,' said Aidan.

Together he and David wrenched the TV away from the wall. The various wires parted company from it, and then Aidan nodded to David, who knew exactly what he meant. Still standing on the buttoned seating, they let the TV fall to the carpet below. Luxuriously thick as it was, it wasn't enough to stop the screen from emitting a satisfying splintering sound as it met the floor.

Daisy clambered onto the padded seat to join her men, and looked over the wall where the broken TV had been. The master craftspeople who built the boat had done a beautiful job, the access hatch for the cables closely fitted, and with no handles. From even a few feet away, the gap was so tiny it would hardly be visible.

But Daisy and her two men had their faces a foot away from it. Aidan looked at David. 'How do we open it?'

'Hmm...' said Daisy, inspecting the tightly-fitting hatch. Then she stood back a little, and thumped the top of it. It sprung away, and David lifted it clear, letting it drop onto the TV on the floor.

'Motion latch,' Daisy grinned, peering inside the small space. It was indeed there to conceal wires and cables. But in Finn's particular boat, it was also concealing something else.

Daisy stepped down, and grinned at the defeated expression on Finn's face. 'I think our job here is done, don't you?'

An officer wrenched Finn's arms behind his back, and clicked handcuffs onto his wrists. Then, a little further away, the helmeted head of another officer appeared in the hatchway from the engine room. He clambered out, then reached both arms back into the space, and half lifted a rag doll up into the stateroom.

'Look what I found in the chain locker!' he said.

Sarah looked like there were no bones in her body. Emotionally drained, clinging onto the officer for support, the vacant eyes in her tearstained face flicked around the room, as her brain tried to accept the freedom it didn't think it would see again. Then she caught sight of Daisy's smiling face, and suddenly she found bones again.

'Oh my god... you're safe,' she cried as they fell into each other's arms.

'And so are you,' said Daisy softly, no longer able to stop the tears from rolling down her cheeks.

'I can't believe it... how?

Daisy sniffed loudly, pressed their faces together. 'I do wish people would stop asking me that. Let's just say I had a little help from an old friend, hey?'

Aidan and David wrapped their arms around the still-hugging women. 'Dad! You're here too!

'Wouldn't miss it for the world,' he said. 'Sometimes miracles do happen...' The words choked to a stop, and his head joined the others in their tearful group hug.

Then they all heard Sarah's muffled whisper. 'It was all so exciting though!'

Then a voice from behind brought the tender moment to an end. 'We would have found it eventually, you know,' said Burrows gruffly. And then he tapped Sarah on the shoulder. 'But well done, you.'

Daisy looked a little disgruntled. 'What about us? Don't we get a tap on the shoulder?'

He turned to glance at them as he headed out to the aft deck. 'I'll deal with you later,' he said, his curt tone filtering through the slight smile on his face.

'I think it's high time we all went and got some rest,' said Daisy.

As they headed back onto the landing stage, police officers seemed to be everywhere. A few of them were rigging up lights on tripod stands, making the whole area around the landing stage as bright as day. They could see Finn being marched to one of the waiting vans. Johnson and Desmond were there too, just about to be loaded into the cages.

Johnson's face was set into a grim, resigned expression. Desmond however, caught sight of them watching as he was being shoved into the van. His face gave nothing away, but although his hands were cuffed, he still somehow managed to stick a single finger up at the elderly woman who should by rights be dead.

The four of them walked slowly to the BMW, flopped their weary bodies into its seats, and Aidan drove back to the cottage. As they pulled into the drive, Daisy glanced back to Sarah and her father in the rear seat. Sarah was fast asleep, her head slumped on her father's shoulder.

'I was going to ask if you guys fancied a quick brandy before you left, but I think I've got my answer.'

David eased his daughter's head from his shoulder. 'Love one, but it'll have to wait until we get home, thanks all the same.'

Somehow, they eased Sarah's semi-conscious body from the car, and got it to the passenger door of David's car. She managed to lift her head, like she'd been drugged almost to unconsciousness, but gave them a broad smile.

'I love you, Daisy,' she whispered, just as David eased her into the seat.

'I love you too, Sarah,' she whispered back.

She felt Aidan's arm around her waist as she just about found the strength to lift an arm to wave the car goodbye. He kissed her on the forehead. 'You sure you've got strength for that brandy?'

'Yes, but it'll have to be in bed... unless you fancy carrying me upstairs.'

Chapter 43

It was eleven-thirty the next morning when the kitchen door was tapped gently, and Maisie's head appeared around it.

'No cooee's this time, Maisie?' Daisy grinned, sitting on her stool at the island unit, still in her dressing gown.

'There's no need to be insulting. I do listen sometimes, you know. I was worried about you.'

'How come?'

'Well, I popped round in the day yesterday, but you weren't here. Then in the evening I passed by when I was taking Brutus for a walk...'

'You take the cat for a walk?' said Daisy incredulously.

'Oh yes. He's very good on the lead, you know. Anyway, when we passed by you still weren't home, so I got to feeling a little worried. All these strange goings-on in the village.'

'Nothing to worry about, dear. We just went for a little sea trip, and came back in a helicopter, that's all.'

'Oh, I see. Well, I don't, not really.'

'No, this time I can understand why you don't. I'll tell you all about it, but mostly we got the bad guys, Maisie. There won't be any goings-on anymore.'

'Oh good. Does that mean I can think things again now?'

Daisy shook her head. 'Welsh Rarebit?'

A slightly shell-shocked Maisie left an hour later, and Daisy and Aidan both knew the news of their adventure would spread around the village faster than a forest fire in a force ten. Despite them telling Maisie to keep it to herself.

Daisy called Sarah on the mobile phone that had made it all possible. She was at the Kings Lynn police station, but just about to go. Burrows had told her to take a few days leave, and spend the time recovering from her ordeal.

She really didn't want to, but her boss could see it was a necessary order, even if she couldn't. But she'd made him promise to keep her informed of developments, and threatened to refuse leave if he didn't agree.

Daisy had to smile at the stubborn streak she recognised all too well. Which she then used to make sure Sarah and her father came for dinner that evening, so they could finally put the whole sorry saga to bed.

There was another reason. Given Sarah's insistence she be kept up to date with developments, Daisy was hoping her boss would keep his word, and by the time she came that evening there would be news to tell.

Just before seven the gravel crunched on the drive. A minute later their guests were walking through the kitchen door, and Sarah was almost bowled over by Daisy's emotional embrace.

She looked her friend over. Compared to the last time she'd seen her, she looked beautiful. But her big blue eyes were lacking their usual sparkle, and Daisy knew from personal experience that the zest for life would take a few days to return.

'Burrows did the right thing, sending you packing for a few days.'

'But...'

'No buts... listen to the voice of experience.'

'Ok boss... I bow to his and your authority.'

'Good. Wine? Not too much mind, or you'll be a rag doll again.'

Yes, mum.'

Aidan served up the beef wellington, a dish he'd decided on with an ironic shake of the head a few hours earlier.

'Don't worry... the beef is nowhere near as pink as the wellies,' he grinned as he cut his guests a few slices.

Sarah looked up from her plate. 'I guess you're both gagging to know if Burrows called me today?'

'As if we would,' Daisy grinned.

'Well, amazingly he did. He probably wanted to make sure I was doing as I was told, this time.'

'I guess you did rather break protocol.'

'That's a polite way of putting it. He told me it was likely going to take me all my days off to write my report. Then he told me I would face disciplinary action.'

'What? After the brilliant and very dangerous things you did?'

'Then he told me he was proud of me, and the disciplinary was just a formality he was going to shove firmly under the carpet.'

Daisy huffed. 'I should think he did. Damn police!'

David smiled. 'As an ex-copper I know these things have to follow procedure, sadly. But Sarah will probably end up getting some kind of commendation.'

'And a promotion?'

'That might be pushing it, for a while at least.'

'Damn police!' Daisy huffed again.

Sarah let out a giggle. 'Don't you want to know what else Burrows told me?'

'Oh yes, We're all ears, trust us.'

'The drugs squad ripped the boat apart, but there were no more drugs. Then again, what you found, Daisy, was a significant haul.'

'That doesn't surprise me. Finn made the trip once a week. He didn't need to bring huge quantities back each time.'

'Precisely. Belgian police have arrested his mother, but it doesn't seem like there will be any evidence to hold her.'

Daisy shook her head. 'She must have known, though. Ah well, one day.'

'Maybe, but it's out of our hands. That one might play for a while yet.'

Daisy filled their glasses. 'Anything closer to home?'

'Oh yes. Finn is squealing like a sewer rat, implicating anyone and everyone except his mother. And when he goes to court, his sentence will be cut.'

'Bugger,' said Aidan.

'Why the hell should it?' said Daisy, narrowing her eyes at Sarah.

'Because he gave Burrows the name of the dealer who had killed Jesse. Apparently he'd called Finn, got his address, went to confront Jesse and things went down just as we'd surmised, Daisy.'

'So you guys got your man, and Finn got off by squealing.'

'Hardly. He's still going down for a very long time.'

'That's something, I suppose.'

'Um... there's something else, guys.'

Daisy had a horrible feeling she knew what was coming. 'He wants to know every detail of our involvement?'

Sarah nodded, still grinning. 'All of it. But right now he's snowed under with sorting out the bad guys, so he's left that particular task to someone else.'

'And who might that be?'

'Me. When I go back to work in four days, interviewing you is my first job.'

226

'Result!' said Daisy.

Daisy and Aidan waved the car goodbye, and then he pulled her close as they stood together in the moonlight, their arms around each other like neither of them wanted to let go. 'Well dear, I think we can say that was a job well done. Beats the Times crossword, anyway!'

'We almost lost our lives though, Dip.'

'But we didn't. We both live to fight another day. And that was just a figure of speech, you understand?'

'Not sure I do, dear.'

'Oh, I'm sure you do, dear. But if you want me to spell it out... now can we please just relax and get back to enjoying our retirement in peace?'

'Well...'

———

We hope you enjoyed 'The Root of All Evil'. We'll be eternally grateful if you can spare two minutes to leave a review on Amazon. It really is very easy, and makes a huge difference; both as feedback to us, and to help potential readers know what others thought.

Thank you so much!

Catch Daisy's second adventure,

'The Strange Case of the Exploding Dolly-trolley'!

Here's a sneaky preview of Book 2...

Chapter 1

Two weeks have passed since Finn and his henchmen were caught red-handed. Two weeks where life seemed to drag itself slowly back to normal. At least, as normal as it ever got where Daisy was concerned.

It had taken her and Aidan the first of those weeks to come to terms with the fact the sting had actually worked, and then to slide gently down the other side of their somewhat dangerous high. As Daisy had said, the day after they got back from Morston Quay... 'Thirty years ago I would have breezed through all that without batting an eyelid. I think I might be getting too old for this, dear.'

Aidan had very gently told her he agreed, but knew better than to use those actual words. He just reminded her she officially retired eleven years ago, and the whole point of moving to the west-Norfolk village of Great Wiltingham was so they could enjoy wilting in peace.

It hadn't sat easily with Daisy, and Mother Nature seemed to confirm the Gods of Destiny were not in accord on that one, with six days of grey cloud and almost-incessant rain making some kind of point. But she finally had to admit they were both right, despite the fact she (and Aidan) would have to put up with itchy feet and even itchier fingers for some months to come.

But reality has a nasty habit of not taking any notice of even the most reluctant of decisions... as they were both about to find out, in a very brutal way.

The days of rain were followed by a week of sunshine and warm September temperatures, and Daisy had just started believing the gods of her destiny were at long last settling down, finally allowing her to have a normal retirement.

Aidan was still sleeping at the cottage. Because of Daisy's previous job and the very unfortunate incident in London three years previously, when they'd moved to the village

229

they bought separate houses. They spent their days together, but mostly when night fell they slept in their own homes.

Despite the fact they'd been married for thirty-five years.

It was Daisy's insistence, with Aidan's reluctant agreement. The unfortunate incident three years ago, when they still lived in London, was connected to her previous employment. In her career in MI6 she'd inevitably made a few enemies. She could easily list a handful of people who might one day seek revenge, at some point when she was perhaps least expecting it.

Three years ago, that revenge came with devastating effect. Daisy and Aidan weren't harmed, but someone very close to them suffered. Their daughter Celia bore the brunt of the retribution, but in a way neither of them expected. And in the kind of way that still didn't have closure.

But the incident was a tragic reminder that Daisy's past could also be her present. At the age of seventy-one, she still found herself wary of every shadow that might turn out to not be a shadow at all.

For two years after the incident she and Aidan fought reluctantly with the options, but eventually it was clear only one alternative stood a chance of working long term. So a year ago they'd moved together but separately to Great Wiltingham, purchasing two houses just a few hundred yards from each other, and putting their wedding rings into a velvet box that never left Daisy's bedside table drawer.

Daisy reverted to her maiden name, and as far as anyone in Norfolk knew, she and Aidan were simply the best of friends. Her previous employers made sure their official records were purged, and their new life of peaceful retirement became a reality.

Aidan had initially protested that Daisy would spend most nights alone, wanting to be there to protect her if the worst happened. But as she pointed out, she was far more equipped to protect herself than he was. In the end he grudgingly accepted that, given the situation, she was probably right.

Aidan had spent his adult life working as an accountant. Daisy hadn't.

For the first year in Great Wiltingham, all was as peaceful as it was intended to be. Daisy played the role of the doddery old biddie to perfection, driving around the village on a mobility scooter, even though she really didn't need to. Then one day, everything changed.

She and Aidan discovered the village was being abused by criminals using it as a delivery-point for hard drugs. Something which, in their case, was way too close to home for comfort.

The identity of the mysterious supplier became an obsession for Daisy. It culminated two weeks ago with him being caught red-handed, with a little help from a young policewoman called Sarah Lowry, who found Daisy's approach to crime-solving way more exciting than mundane police work!

Then, two weeks of relative peace later, life had returned to something approaching normal. But their scary adventure had brought changes. Although the bad guys were nothing to do with the enemies Daisy had made in the past, they brought her a strange, unexpected kind of nervousness. Aidan had moved in while the sting was under way, and fourteen days after it was over, he still hadn't moved out.

Daisy was getting used to shuggling up with him at night. So much so that three days ago, she'd ever-so-vaguely suggested they might have been wrong to buy separate houses. But as usual, it came out in Daisy-speak. Which didn't fool Aidan for a second...

'Dear, I've been thinking,' she said quietly, sitting on her stool at the island unit in the kitchen, eating her comfort food of cheese on toast with added pepperoni and jalapenos.

'Should I be worried?' he grinned.

'Maybe. You seem to be enjoying sleeping here.'

'I thought you'd never ask.'

'I haven't asked anything yet.'

'Haven't you?' He put an arm around her shoulders, and gave her a gentle kiss, which was only slightly jalapeno-flavoured.

'No fooling you, is there?'

'I do have a brain the size of a small galaxy, according to you.'

She took a sip of the coffee, trying not to grin. 'Maybe sleeping in separate houses has outlived its usefulness.'

'It was never useful, just necessary. And annoying.'

'Ok, galactic-brain. So you've sussed me. What are you going to do about it?'

'You leaving the decision to me?'

'Yes dear.'

So this morning, Aidan had left at nine to meet the estate agent at the bungalow, and be there while they planted the 'For Sale' board. At nine-thirty, Daisy wandered across the gravel drive and opened the white five-barred gate. Robert James, the service agent in Kings Lynn, was coming at ten to take her mobility scooter away for service, and with the gate open, he could drive his van straight in.

She was just about to head back inside when she heard a cheerful 'Coo-eee', and turned back to the road to see Maisie walking past, waving manically. 'Lovely morning, Daisy.'

She wandered over to the little gate next to the big gate. 'Out for a constitutional, Maisie?' she said, and then saw her friend wasn't alone.

Maisie was widely regarded as the dottiest resident in the village. Some even saw her as the village crazie, but in reality she wasn't crazy at all. Rather eccentric maybe, and bordering on acute dottiness... a fact borne out by the fact she was passing by taking her cat for a walk.

Daisy tried not to giggle at the strange sight of the furball on a red lead. 'Yes, Maisie, it is a lovely morning. Taking Brutus for a walk I see.'

'Oh yes. He's not been out for a few days, you know.'

'But you put him out every night.'

'I know, but it's not the same. He likes his walks on the leash.'

'So I see,' Daisy said, quite astonished to see Brutus standing dutifully quietly by his owner's side. 'I have to say, he is good on the lead...'

Maisie looked quite indignant. 'Of course he is. I did train him well you know. When I got up this morning, he was a bit spooked. He even hissed at me. He soon calmed down after I gave him a bit of fillet steak and promised to take him for a walk. Anyway, I'm now going. He'll be needing a pee soon, and I haven't refilled his cat tray yet.'

Daisy tried to keep the amused shake of her head from Maisie's line of sight, but her dotty friend was already

233

walking away, so it wasn't that difficult. 'I guess you trained him not to pee up lampposts then?' she called after the slightly-portly woman in the polyester skirt and patterned blouse.

She looked back and tut-tutted. 'Daisy, sometimes I wonder about you. He's a cat!'

Chapter 2

Daisy headed back into the kitchen, and picked up the keys to the dolly-trolley, the mobility scooter affectionately christened by Aidan when he modified it to go faster than any dolly-trolley ever had. She'd decided to move it out of its little open-fronted enclosure sitting next to the garage, so it would be sitting waiting for Robert to drive it straight into his van when he arrived.

She didn't quite make it. As she walked across the drive towards the enclosure, a car turned into the open gateway, and the cheerful toot of the horn was accompanied by an even more cheerful smile. Daisy turned on her heels just before she reached the enclosure, and walked over to the car.

The young woman dressed in the pristine police uniform dropped the driver's window, and smiled a warm smile. Her big blue eyes seemed to sparkle in the morning sunlight, and the flawless skin on her pretty face appeared to glow with vitality.

She looked a million miles from the limp rag doll who had struggled out of the engine room of Finn's boat two weeks ago. In all fairness, she had just been through thirty-six hours of stowaway hell. Daisy knew all too well it took a week or two to recover from ordeals like that.

'I wasn't expecting to see you today, Sarah,' she smiled.

'Not stopping. On my way to the station, later shift today. Just wanted to tell you Burrows read your eight-page interview report we almost-truthfully wrote. Then he sighed like he didn't really believe most of it, and told me it would be filed away and ignored.'

'That was good of your boss,' said Daisy, only slightly-sarcastically.

'Quite honestly he's got so much on right now, with organising the case with the CPS so that murderers and drug runners get their due sentences, he's not got time to bother about a couple of nosy old cronies like you two.'

It was said with a smile, and taken the same way. 'I bet the grumpy DCI wishes he had got the time though... I can just imagine the delight on his face when he reads us the riot act and tells us to leave police business to the police in future.'

'Yeah well, Daisy. Maybe if he'd had the time it might have been the best thing?'

Daisy let out a huge, genuine sigh. 'I know. I'm too old for those kind of shenanigans, as everyone keeps telling me... including my own gut.'

'Somehow I wonder if you'll truly listen to it, or to everyone else.'

'It's hard, Sarah... so hard. You got time for a coffee?'

'Wish I had. Gotta get to the station. Thanks anyway. We still on for dinner tomorrow?'

'You bet. Aidan is rooting through his cookbooks to find something special.'

'He's a good man. Taking care of you as he does, and then having to go home every night?'

It was a question, a leading one. Designed to provoke a certain reply. It came.

'Actually, he's not going home anymore. He's round at the bungalow now, supervising the planting of the sale board. He decided two houses were a bit silly.'

'He decided?'

'Well...'

Sarah grinned. 'I'm delighted for you both. It's the right thing. I'm glad you asked him to stay permanently.'

'Um... I...' Daisy started to protest at the inference, but then realised there were no words to argue with. Sarah had got it spot on.

The window whirred up, and with a cheery and slightly self-satisfied wave, she backed out of the drive and drove away. Five seconds later, Robert's van was backing in. He pulled up next to Daisy, and opened the driver's door.

'Mornin', Flower,' he grinned cheerily. He was the only person other than Aidan to call her that. In his early sixties and a true Norfolk boy, he was close to retirement, but rather like Daisy wasn't exactly looking forward to it. Mobility scooters were his life, and the vast majority of his customers were those who, unlike Daisy, actually needed his help.

'Morning, Bob. You want a coffee before you go?' she smiled to him.

'I shouldn't, got a lot on today. But if you be twisting my arm...'

'I'll put the kettle on.' She glanced down to the keys in her hand. 'I was just about to pull it out for you, but Sarah came, and then you were here.'

'No worries. I'll drive it into the van while you make that coffee.'

236

He opened the rear doors, and pressed the button to drop the tail-lift. Daisy handed him the keys, and headed into the kitchen to fill the kettle. Aidan would be back any time, so she made sure she boiled enough water for him too.

Through the open side window she heard the crunch of boots on gravel, and knew Robert was heading to the enclosure to fetch the dolly-trolley. For a second she thought about hurrying out to remind him Aidan had modified the top speed somewhat, on her insistence that it didn't go fast enough. But then she realised it was too late anyway, as the whirr of the motor told her he was already driving it out of the enclosure.

Three seconds later, another sound filled her ears. An ear-splitting noise, which drowned out everything else for a single, devastating second.

A loud explosion reverberated around the driveway, and shook the house to its very foundations.

————

Catch Daisy Morrow: 'The Strange Case of the Exploding Dolly-trolley', and find out what's happened!

It's available exclusively on Amazon

And why not give our brand new series a go?
The Sandie Shaw Mysteries is a 1920's mystery series set in Chicago

When Sandie witnesses her client committing a cut-and-dried murder, her head tells her to walk away. Her heart tells her she can't. It's a life-changing decision...

———

AND DO COME AND JOIN US!

We'd love you to become a VIP Reader.

Our intro library is the most generous in publishing!
Join our mail list and grab it all for free.
We really do appreciate every single one of you,
so there's always a freebie or two coming along,
news and updates, advance reads of new releases...

Go here to get started...
rtgreen.net

Printed in Great Britain
by Amazon